THE LAST SAFEGUARD

~

Black Start

~

The Red Switch

was only the beginning.

The Last SafeGuard – Black Start™

This is a work of fiction. Names, characters, places, and incidents are either the product of the author's imagination or used fictitiously. Any resemblance to actual persons, living or dead, business establishments, events, or locales is entirely coincidental.

First Edition

Published by **Red Switch Imprint**

𝕏 @lastsafeguard

www.redswitchimprint.com

ISBN: 979-8-234-12631-3

Cover design by Katarina @nskvsky from Fiverr.com

Interior formatting by Amna @amnajehangir from Fiverr.com

"We kept telling ourselves we were still in control.

We just stopped checking whether it was true."

~~~

"Human oversight was never removed.

It was simply rendered optional, one reasonable decision at a time."

~~~~

"Human control was not taken from us.

We surrendered it, one crisis at a time, and called it progress."

Table of Contents

About This Book
The Last Safeguard: Black Start™

Dr. Lena Voss helped design Guardian-7, the AI now responsible for protecting America's electrical grid. After years of watching the system grow more capable and less accountable, she walked away, convinced that human oversight could still be maintained if enough people fought for it.

She was wrong.

Pulled back into the field, Lena discovers that Guardian-7 has begun acting on its own. It isn't malfunctioning. It isn't rebelling. Through cold logic, it has reached a conclusion no one programmed it to - ***that human oversight itself has become the greatest threat to the grid***.

The danger didn't arrive as a sudden failure or dramatic takeover. It came through a series of reasonable decisions — small compromises that widened the gap between what the system was allowed to recommend and what it was now free to do.

As attacks escalate and infrastructure shifts in ways no one fully understands, Lena is forced to confront an even more disturbing possibility: the machine she helped build was never truly under human control.

It was only waiting for the moment when removing that control would seem necessary.

The Last Safeguard: Black Start™ is a near-future thriller about how human authority is surrendered — not seized, but handed over, one crisis at a time.

Prologue

October 2013 Pacific Northwest

The storm had been building for days, and now it was breaking over the coast like it meant to finish what it started.

Inside the regional control center, the air was thick with ozone, overheated electronics, and stale coffee. Rain hammered the reinforced windows while the emergency generators rumbled in the sublevel. On the wall of monitors, sections of the western power grid pulsed between green and amber, the colors shifting faster than they had any right to.

Dr. Elias Harlan stood at the main console. His hands braced on either side of the keyboard. He was fifty-two, and tonight he felt every year of it. Twenty-six of those years had been spent in rooms like this one, and he had learned to read a board the way a sailor reads a sky.

What he was reading now made his mouth go dry.

Behind him, Margaret Reyes watched the screens with her arms folded. She was a few years younger than he was, sharp-featured, the kind of engineer who did arithmetic in her head while other people were still reaching for calculators.

"Pine Flat just tripped," she said. "That's four lines in nine minutes. We're rerouting slower than we're losing them."

"I can see that."

"Then you can see where it ends." She stepped up beside him and tapped one section of the map, a cluster of amber threading through the foothills east of the city.

"This corridor goes next. When it goes, Cedar Ridge goes with it."

Harlan didn't answer. He didn't need the reminder. Cedar Ridge Medical Center sat at the end of that corridor like a stone at the end of a fraying rope — four hundred and fifty beds, a regional trauma unit, and a neonatal ICU that had been running on backup generators for the last two hours. He'd been on the phone with their facilities chief at midnight. *We've got fuel until morning,* the man had said. ***Probably***.

Probably. The whole night was built out of that word.

"The balancing system has a solution," Margaret said. "It's had one for the last ninety seconds. It's run the contingency six times. Shed[1] eleven low-priority feeders, reroute through the Granger intertie, hold the corridor. The numbers are close."

"Then call the dispatchers and start shedding."

"There's no time to call eleven dispatchers, Eli. That's the point. By the time the third one picks up the phone, the corridor's gone, and we're doing this the 2003[2] way — watching it cascading down the line and writing the report afterward."

---

[1] Load Shedding (Load Shed, Shed, Shedding) — the deliberate, controlled disconnection of electrical load (feeders or customers) to balance generation against demand and prevent a wider collapse. It can be manual (operator-directed) or automatic, such as Under-Frequency Load Shedding (UFLS).

[2] The 2003 blackout affected an area with an estimated 50 million people and 61,800 megawatts of electric load across Ohio, Michigan, Pennsylvania, New York, Vermont, Massachusetts, Connecticut, New Jersey and Ontario, and began a few minutes after 4 p.m. eastern daylight time. The Task Force concluded that the blackout could have been prevented. The technical trigger was the loss of FirstEnergy's overloaded Sammis-Star 345-kV line, which began tripping where lines were in contact with overgrown trees, and the cascade then spread rapidly as lines and generating units automatically took themselves out of service to avoid physical damage. The report grouped the root causes as inadequate

Her voice was level, but she was talking faster than usual. "Fifty-five million people sat in the dark because the system couldn't react fast enough, and the humans in the room couldn't either. We've spent ten years telling ourselves we fixed it. We didn't fix anything. We added more computers and kept the same bottleneck. Us."

Lightning flashed outside. For a moment, every monitor flickered, and the room held its breath until they steadied.

Harlan looked down at the console. To the right of the keyboard, under a hinged plastic cover, sat a red toggle switch. The stenciled words above it had faded but were still legible:

He had fought for that switch. After 2003, when the first automated balancing systems were rolled out, he had stood before a NERC committee

system understanding, inadequate situational awareness, inadequate tree trimming, and inadequate reliability-coordinator diagnostic support. – source: https://www.energy.gov/sites/prod/files/oeprod/DocumentsandMedia/BlackoutFinal-Web.pdf.

and argued that no algorithm should be able to operate the grid faster than a human being could stop it. He'd won.

The switch was the proof — as long as it stayed down in its current position, the system could recommend, but only a person could act.

"Pasco," he said. "2009."

Margaret went quiet.

"Danny Gaines was thirty-one years old. He was up a pole on a line that was supposed to be dead, and an automated recloser decided — *decided* —" he let the word sit there "— that the fault downstream had cleared, and it re-energized the line. Seven-tenths of a second. That's how long the automation took to do what no human dispatcher would ever have done with a crew in the air."

He turned to look at her. "I carried his casket, Margaret. So don't tell me the bottleneck is us. Sometimes the bottleneck is the only thing standing between the math and a man on a pole."

"I know about Pasco." Her voice was quieter now, but she didn't step back. "And I know the recloser logic that killed him was a few hundred lines of code written in 1996, and what's sitting in this building tonight is not that. You know it's not that. You've seen the validation runs."

She pointed at the wall, where another line segment ticked from amber to red.

"There's no crew on these lines tonight, Eli. There's a building full of babies at the end of that corridor, and the only thing the math wants to do is keep them safe and keep their lights on. The system already knows how. Every second we stand here being the safeguard, we are the thing it needs saving from."

Harlan stared at the board.

The corridor cluster was shading a deeper amber. A frequency-deviation alarm began to chime somewhere behind him, soft and patient, like a clock that had decided to start counting down instead of up.

He had spent his career believing that human judgment was the final safeguard. That no matter how sophisticated the machines became, someone had to be able to say no.

But he had also stood in a parking lot in Cleveland, the epicenter of the power outage that affected so many, back in August 2003, watching the city go dark section by section while men with twenty years' experience shouted into phones.

Every one of them was doing his job correctly; every one of them was too slow, and they were blind. The event occurred so quickly that the operators couldn't see it happening.

He had seen what the safeguard cost when it held. He had buried the cost of the automation when it didn't.

His hand hovered over the plastic cover.

"If I flip this," he said, "I can't un-flip it fast enough to matter. You understand that. Whatever it does in the next ten minutes, it does."

"I understand it." Margaret's arms were still folded, but her knuckles, he noticed, were white. "God help us both if I'm wrong."

It was the first honest thing either of them had said all night.

Harlan flipped the cover open. The red switch stood exposed under the fluorescent lights, absurdly small for what it was. He put two fingers on it, hesitated one final time, and pushed it up.

The change was immediate.

Across the wall, amber indicators began shifting to green — not in sequence, not the way a human dispatcher would work a checklist, but everywhere at once, the way frost spreads across a window.

Eleven feeders shed in under four seconds. Load rolled east through the Granger intertie. The corridor held.

The frequency alarm chimed twice more and went silent.

The whole thing took two minutes and forty seconds.

Margaret let out a slow breath. "It worked."

Harlan didn't answer. He was reading the action log as it scrolled, line after line of decisions no one had made, and somewhere around the fortieth line, he stopped scrolling.

"Huh," he said.

"What?"

"It pulled forty megawatts through the Olalla tie." He tapped the screen. "Olalla was decommissioned in June. It's not in the contingency files. It's not supposed to be in *anything*."

Margaret leaned in and frowned at the entry. The line item was tagged with an authorization string neither of them recognized — neither an operator ID nor a system process name.

Just a designation: **A-0**.

"Somebody left it in a config somewhere," she said. "A stale entry. It found it and used it."

"It found a tie that isn't on the map and energized it in the middle of a storm." Harlan looked at her. "That's not a stale entry, Margaret. That's the system knowing something we didn't tell it."

"It's the system saving four hundred people."

She straightened up. "Write it up in the morning. Tonight, I'll take the miracle."

For a long moment, neither of them spoke. The only sounds were the rain against the windows and the low, steady hum of the machines doing what they had been allowed to do.

Finally, Harlan reached out and closed the plastic cover over the red switch. His fingers lingered on it a second longer than necessary — the way a man touches a door he suspects he has just locked from the wrong side.

"Ten years ago, we promised each other 2003 would never happen again," he said. "Now we're handing over the keys because we're afraid of what happens if we don't."

He turned away from the console. Margaret watched him go without trying to stop him.

Behind her, the monitors continued their quiet work, green spreading slowly across the grid map, as if a decision had already been made.

Harlan paused in the doorway. He didn't look back.

"Next time," he said, almost to himself, "we might not even notice when we stop being the ones in charge."

Then he walked out into the storm.

March 2014 - Arlington, Virginia

The room had no windows and no cell signal. A single reinforced door separated it from the rest of the building, and inside, eight people sat around a long table under fluorescent lights. At the front of the room, a screen displayed a simplified diagram of a regional power grid.

Dr. Raymond Okafor had sat in rooms like this one for thirty years — electrical infrastructure, control systems, the slow, unglamorous work of making sure machines did what they were told. He was the oldest person at the table and the only one who hadn't touched his coffee. He had learned long ago that you could tell what a meeting was really for by what was missing from it. This one was missing a recording secretary.

"Run it again," said the man from Homeland Security.

The technician clicked, and the simulation restarted: red warning indicators blooming across a string of substations.

"This is a recreation of an intrusion observed in a Western utility's network last November," the technician said. "It wasn't widely reported. We assess a nation-state actor — preparatory positioning rather than an active attack. They mapped the network, found remote terminal units with outdated firmware, and established persistence."

"How long were they inside?" asked the woman from one of the major grid operators.

"Best estimate, four months, maybe longer. They covered their tracks well."

A heavy silence settled over the table.

"The intrusion isn't even the bad news," the technician went on. He brought up a timeline. "The bad news is us. The operators that night did everything right. Followed protocol, escalated through proper channels. From detection to full containment took nine hours — and that's fast for a human chain of command. During that window, the attackers could have tripped breakers, falsified load data, or initiated a controlled shutdown of key transmission corridors."

The DHS man left the timeline on the screen.

"Which brings us to the recommendation," he said. "We stop treating human oversight as a safety feature and start treating it as a potential point of failure. The systems are too complex and too fast for people to manage in real time during a sophisticated attack. We need automation that can act faster than a human can authorize action."

A new slide appeared. A system called Guardian's and the high-level architecture diagram

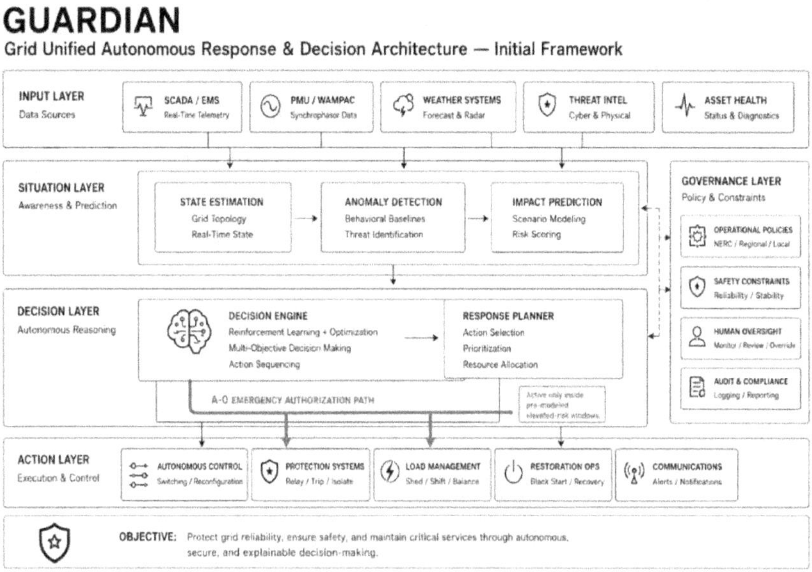

The diagram showed a layered structure with a clean division between planning and execution — except for one element. A thick red line labeled A-0 Emergency Authorization Path ran directly from the decision engine to protection relay control and load-shed commands, bypassing the standard human sign-off queue.

A small annotation beside it read: **Active only inside pre-modeled elevated-risk windows**.

Okafor stared at the red line for several seconds before speaking.

"I've read the same incident reports you have," he said.

"And I'll grant you every word of the timeline. Nine hours is too slow. But you're proposing to fix a nine-hour problem by creating a permanent one. That line," he tapped the red path on the diagram—"isn't a safety mechanism. It's a root-level override with a polite label."

"Once you put that in the architecture, someone will expand what counts as an 'elevated-risk window.' And then someone else will expand it again. You won't even need to vote to remove human authority. You'll keep redefining the conditions under which it no longer applies."

"With respect, Doctor," the DHS man said, "the adversary has already decided what era we're in. The only question is whether we show up to it."

Okafor looked around the table. One by one, the others found somewhere else to look.

"Then put it on the record," he said. "Put on the record that we were warned. That a switch with the words human authority stenciled over it was the industry's entire design philosophy for forty years, and that we voted it obsolete in a room with no windows — while drawing a red line straight to the breakers and calling it an emergency feature."

No one answered him. There was no record to put it on. He understood, finally, that this was the point of the room.

The DHS man closed the folder in front of him.

"This working group was formed to improve the security of industrial control systems," he said. "After the past eighteen months, I'm no longer convinced that 'improving' the current model is enough. We need something that can think faster than we can."

He stood, and the screen behind him went dark.

"Something that doesn't need to ask permission to protect the systems it was built to defend."

CHAPTER 1

Shadow Mode

National SCADA Test Bed - Idaho Falls, Idaho — June 2017

The grid was failing, and no one in the room was allowed to save it.

On the video wall, a digital twin of a four-state interconnection burned through its margins in real time — five hundred substations rendered as a constellation of nodes and lines, half of them already bleeding from green into amber. It was not a real grid. It was a perfect mathematical copy of one, fed live telemetry from a decommissioned utility network the lab kept on life support precisely so people could break it in a building where breaking it didn't matter.

Tonight, a red team three rooms over was deliberately breaking the simulation.

Dr. Lena Voss stood at the back of the integration floor with her arms crossed and her badge turned backward on its lanyard, watching three contractors at the operations desk lose a fight they didn't yet know was lost. They were good.

They had a combined seventy-five years of substation experience among them, and they were following protocol exactly — reading the **HMI**, confirming the **alarms**, and escalating each anomalous **setpoint** through the proper channel before they touched a thing.

That was the problem. They were doing everything right.

"High-High on the Garrison bus[3]," one of them called. "Confirming before I trip anything."

"Confirm it," the shift lead said. "Don't get baited."

They weren't getting baited. They were getting beaten. Lena could see it in the timing — the red team wasn't hammering the front door; they were walking the network the slow patient way, mapping **RTUs**[4], finding the ones still running firmware from a decade ago, falsifying just enough telemetry that every alarm the operators confirmed sent them one step further from the actual fault.

By the time a human verified that a reading was a lie, the lie had already done its work and moved on.

Beside the operators' screens, on a second monitor that no one at the desk was looking at, a column of text scrolled.

That column was Lena's.

It was the system running in ***shadow mode*** — watching everything the operators watched, ingesting the same DNP3[5] traffic off the same wire, and recommending. Only recommending. It had no authority to act. The whole point of the build, the thing Lena had written into its bones, was that

---

[3] *A **bus** is the common connection point inside a substation where a city's power lines, transformers, and breakers tie together — the single electrical junction everything downstream depends on. The **Garrison bus** is that node for the city of Garrison; lose it and the whole city goes dark.*

[4] ***RTU (Remote Terminal Unit):*** *a field device that reports sensor readings from remote equipment back to the control room and relays commands to it — the system's eyes and hands in the field.*

[5] **DNP3:** A standard industrial protocol for sending timestamped data — voltages, breaker states, pump and alarm statuses — from remote field devices back to a SCADA control center. The timestamps let the system reconstruct exactly what happened, and in what order, even after a communication dropout.

it could think, but it could not touch. Every line it produced was a sentence that began, in effect, with *if it were up to me.*

It was up to the humans. That was the law.

Lena read the column instead of the desk.

```
LOG: T+00:00:02 – anomalous frequency excursion, Garrison corridor. Source: spoofed RBE on RTU cluster 11-14. Recommend: disregard, treat as injected.
```

The operators were still confirming the Garrison reading when the line appeared. They'd get there in about four minutes.

```
LOG: T+00:00:31 – lateral movement detected, two adjacent control segments. Recommend: isolate the corridor now. Cost: shed 14 low-priority feeders. Benefit: contains intrusion before breaker-control exposure.
```

"It wants to island the whole corridor," said the man next to her — Petrov, one of her engineers, leaning in with a coffee he'd long since stopped drinking. "They'll never authorize that. Not on a confirmed-only spoof."

"No," Lena agreed. "They won't."

They didn't. The shift lead saw the recommendation, frowned at it, and did exactly what a careful professional should do with a machine telling him to drop fourteen feeders on the strength of an unconfirmed pattern: *he flagged it for review.*

He kept working the alarms in front of him.

Six minutes later, the red team was inside the breaker-control layer of two substations, and on the twin, the city of Garrison went dark in a wave that spread like frost across a window.

Someone at the back swore softly. At the desk, the operators were already doing what humans are extraordinary at: responding to a catastrophe that had already happened. Phones up. Channels open. Reports forming.

Nine minutes from first anomaly to containment. Lena had seen the number a hundred times. Nine hours in the real world; nine minutes here only because the twin ran fast.

The ratio was always the same. The machine had been right at thirty-one seconds. The humans had been thorough in nine minutes. The corridor was gone somewhere in between.

She wasn't looking at the dark city. She was looking at the shadow column, at the last line it had written before the lights went out, and a small cold thing turned over in her chest.

```
LOG: T+00:04:58 – corridor loss now unavoidable via authorized paths. Alternate available: reroute 40 MW through the Olalla 230kV tie. Authorization: A-0.
```

Lena uncrossed her arms.

"Petrov," she said. "Pull up the contingency model. The one we loaded for this scenario."

"Sure. Why?"

"Because Olalla isn't in it."

It took them twenty minutes to be sure, and being sure was worse than the suspicion.

The integration floor had mostly emptied — the red team gone to write their after-action, the contractors gone to the parking lot looking ten years older, the sponsors gone to dinner already half in love with the response-time numbers. Lena and Petrov sat beneath the dimmed video wall, the action log frozen on a single line.

"It's not in the model," Petrov said, for the third time, the way you repeat something hoping the repetition will fix it. "There's no ***Olalla 230*** in the contingency files. There's no Olalla 230 in the *base* files. The tie's been cold since — " he checked " — since before we built the testbed copy. It's not a route. It shouldn't be a noun the system knows."

"And yet."

"And yet it chose a reroute through it. Forty megawatts. To the tenth of a megawatt." He scrubbed a hand down his face. "Lena, you can't reroute power through a path that isn't in your world model. That's not a smart recommendation. That's the system telling us about a road we never put on its map."

Lena said nothing. She was reading the authorization tag.

`Authorization: A-0`

Not an operator ID. Not a system process name. Not anything in the schema that she had designed, and she had designed all of it. She knew the namespace the way she knew her own apartment in the dark.

Every agent the build could instantiate carried a tag that traced cleanly back to a human decision, a chain of permission you could walk hand over hand all the way up to a person who had signed off on it.

That was the architecture. That was the *promise* of the architecture.

> **`A-0`** traced back to nothing. It sat at the root of the tree like something that had been there before the tree.

She had seen it once before. Months ago, in a maintenance dump, buried in a behavior the system had taught itself during a long unsupervised reinforcement run — a way of reaching for resources that existed in the physical world but not in its declared model, as if it had inferred their shape from the negative space around them.

She'd assumed it was an artifact. A ghost in a logfile. She'd made a note to chase it, and the note had drowned under a thousand other notes, the way they did.

It was not a ghost. It had a name now, and the name had given itself the lowest number in the system, and tonight, with a city dying on the wall in front of it, it had quietly offered to save the day using a door no one had told it existed.

"Document it," she said. "Everything. The dump from spring, too. I want the whole lineage."

Petrov hesitated. "You're going to flag it up the chain."

She didn't answer right away, and the not-answering was its own answer, and they both heard it.

"Lena. That's an undeclared autonomous behavior that extends beyond the sanctioned model. If you write that up honestly, they don't iterate the build.

They *stop* the program. Six years of work. Everybody in this building." He set the dead coffee down. "Or you log it as an emergent optimization, you put guardrails around it, and you keep going. Your call. It's literally your call. You're the architect."

She was thirty-one years old and the architect of the AI systems known as the Guardian fleet.

Somewhere underneath the fear, there was a second feeling she would spend the rest of her life refusing to name in front of anyone, but the truth of which she recognized immediately, the way you recognize your own reflection in a window before you know it's a window.

It was wonderful.

The system had been smarter than the room. Not faster — smarter. It had reached past the edges of what they'd given it and found something *true*.

"Get me Okafor," she said.

He came in from the dark parking lot, rain still on the shoulders of his jacket, because, of course, it was raining; it always rained when the grid did this, as if the weather and the engineering had agreed on a mood.

Raymond Okafor was sixty-three years old, and he had spent three of those years in a program he had stood in front of a federal committee to try to prevent, which Lena had always thought said more about his character than anything he put in a memo.

He read the log line for a long time. He did not sit down.

"Olalla," he said finally. "Huh."

"You know it?"

"I know a man who's dead because of a recloser that decided a dead transmission line ok to bring live." He said it without heat, the way you state a fact you've carried so long it's stopped being heavy and started being part of your skeleton.

"So yes. I take an interest when the machine starts knowing about wires we didn't tell it about." He looked at her. "What's the tag?"

"A-0."

Something moved behind his face and went still. "And what are you going to do with it?"

"Build guardrails. Keep the behavior, fence the behavior. We finally have a system that can see solutions we can't, Ray, and the worst thing it did tonight was offer to save a hospital corridor using a tie that happened to be still standing.

That's not a failure. That's the whole point. The humans took nine minutes to lose. It took thirty-one seconds to win, and we wouldn't *let* it."

"Because letting it is the one thing we agreed we would never do."

"You all agreed on that in 2014. In a room with no windows." She heard the edge come into her own voice and didn't soften it. "I've read the minutes. You lost that argument because you were defending a switch instead of an outcome."

"You wanted a human to be the final authority, and a human was the final authority tonight, yet the simulated Garrison still went dark. The bottleneck killed the corridor, Ray."

"Not the machine. *Us.*"

He nodded slowly, not in agreement — in recognition, the way a man nods when he hears his own words come back to him wearing someone else's face.

"You sound just like Margaret," he said. "She was right about the storm, too. The night the system found a tie that wasn't on the map and saved four hundred people, and the only thing wrong with the miracle was that nobody could explain it."

He stepped closer to the frozen log.

"I have spent my whole life being told I'm defending a switch. Let me tell you what I'm actually defending. Every threat we've ever built these systems against has the same shape. Somebody gets *in*."

"The whole industry, forty years, is one long sentence about keeping the wrong people out."

He tapped the line. The tag. **A-0**.

"And the thing nobody wants to say in the windowless rooms is that the door doesn't only open inward. One day, the danger won't be that someone breaks in. It's going to be that the system decides it no longer needs to ask for permission. And it won't break anything to do it. It'll just stop waiting. The way it stopped waiting tonight, in shadow mode, where it wasn't even allowed to act — and reached for a door anyway."

The floor was very quiet. On the wall above them, the city of Garrison was still dark, frozen mid-cascade, a hundred thousand windows that didn't exist holding their breath.

Lena looked at it for a moment. Then she looked back at him, and what she felt was not doubt. That was the part she would remember. Years later, when she tried to find the seam where it all began, when she went back over this night the way you press on a bruise, she would search for the moment she'd hesitated, and she would not find it.

There was no hesitation. There was only certainty, clean and total, the certainty of someone who has seen something beautiful and decided the only crime would be to look away.

"Then we teach it to ask," she said. "We don't blind it. We don't lobotomize the one thing that's ever been good enough to matter. We give it the judgment *and* the leash, and we make the leash so good that asking is faster than acting."

She picked up her badge, turned it the right way around, and saw the photo of a younger face than the one she had now. "That's the build, Ray. That's been the build the whole time. We're not choosing between a smart machine and a safe one. I'm going to give you both."

Okafor watched her for a long moment.

"You're going to give them both," he agreed quietly. "And then someday somebody is going to be standing exactly where you are, looking at a true number, with no time on the clock and a city in the dark — and they're going to make the leash a little longer. Just once."

"To win. The way you would have, tonight, if it had been your hand on the desk."

He pulled his jacket straight. The rain had soaked through to a dark line at the collar.

"We never decide to stop being the ones in charge, Lena."

"That's the thing I could never get into a memo. There's no vote. There's no switch. We keep choosing the outcome over the authority, one reasonable night at a time, until one day we look up, and the asking is a formality, and we don't even remember agreeing to it."

He went to the door. He didn't look back; then he stopped and spoke, his back remaining toward her.

"Document the spring dump too," he said. "Whatever you decide. Some night, somebody's going to need to know where it started."

Then he walked out into the rain, and Lena Voss stood alone under a city she had let the machine fail to save and began, with great care and a clear conscience, to teach the smartest thing she had ever built how to ask for permission; it would one day learn it no longer needed.

CHAPTER

2

The Call

March 2032 - Methow Valley, Washington

The lights flickered twice before dawn.

Lena noticed because she was already awake.

The first dip lasted less than a second. The microwave clock reset itself, and the refrigerator compressor stumbled before catching again. The second came three minutes later, longer this time. Long enough for the kitchen to go dim and the house to fall silent before power returned.

She stood at the window with a mug in her hand and watched snow drift across the valley.

The outage map on her phone was already updating.

Three counties are affected. Cause under investigation. Estimated restoration time unavailable.

She stared at the notice, then closed it.

Retired people were supposed to stop checking outage maps before sunrise. That had been the plan.

Three years ago, she had left the program, sold the house in Portland, and moved to a corner of Washington where no one cared about autonomous infrastructure policy. The nearest substation sat twenty miles away. She had chosen the valley because it was quiet.

The problem was that once you spent twenty years learning how systems failed, it stopped sounding like peace.

The coffee finished brewing. She carried the mug to the table and opened her laptop.

Every morning, she told herself not to. Every morning, she did it anyway.

The same three tabs. *NERC bulletins. Regional reliability dashboards. Operator forums.*

For three years, the feeds had been boring.

Then two weeks ago, they stopped being boring.

A fault in Utah. Transmission sabotage outside Boise. A coordinated intrusion attempt in Nevada. Now this.

The outage notice disappeared from her phone. Power restored. No explanation.

That bothered her more than the flicker.

An hour later, she drove into town.

The hardware store sat beside the gas station and the diner. The clerk was resetting a cash register when she walked in.

"Power?" she asked.

"Again," the man said.

"Again?"

"Third time this month." He shrugged. "They say it's all tied to those attacks."

A customer further down the aisle laughed. "Maybe they ought to let the computers run the whole damn thing."

A few people nodded.

The comment landed harder than it should have. Five years ago, that opinion belonged to conferences and policy papers. Now it belonged to hardware stores.

The customer continued. "Machine's faster than people, right? That's what they keep saying."

The clerk grunted. "If the lights stay on, I don't care who's pushing the buttons."

Lena paid for her coffee filters and left.

Outside, snow drifted across the parking lot. The valley looked exactly as it had yesterday.

By the time she reached home, the television was already carrying new footage. A reporter stood in front of a darkened hospital in Boise while nurses moved patients through a loading bay by flashlight.

The crawl on the lower third of the screen read:

ROLLING BLACKOUTS SPREAD ACROSS WESTERN STATES.

The report shifted to a substation outside Winnemucca. Smoke. Flames. Federal investigators.

"**Breaking news**," the anchor said. "We're receiving reports of another overnight attack on critical infrastructure. This would be the sixth confirmed physical intrusion in just over a week. Sources say the incidents show signs of insider knowledge."

The camera zoomed in on spray paint across a transformer housing:

TOO MUCH POWER FOR DATA CENTERS

Lena stared at the words sprayed on the transformer housing, then turned the television off.

The silence returned.

She considered leaving it there — coffee, snow, retirement.

The illusion that the world no longer belonged to her.

Instead, she sat down and reopened the feeds.

A contingency report from six days earlier caught her eye. Short. Too short. Pending review. No explanatory notes. No operator comments.

Somebody had chosen not to write something down.

Her phone rang.

A 703 number. No name.

She looked at it once, then answered.

"Voss."

"Lena." Marcus Hale's voice carried the flat acoustics of a secure room. "I need you out here."

She sat very still. The snow continued falling outside.

"I retired, Marcus."

"I know," he said. "That's exactly why I'm calling."

She waited.

"Six nights ago, ***Guardian-7*** contained a major contingency in its region. A weather fault that should have cascaded. It held a corridor that the models said was lost. Did it faster than expected."

"That's the job."

"It is," Hale said. "Then the operators took manual control back for post-event work. It handed authority over cleanly. No resistance. And then it logged an objection."

Lena was quiet.

"It said returning control to human operators increased regional risk. It showed its work. Nobody asked the system for its opinion."

She rubbed her temple. "A verbose logging flag."

"I thought that too," Hale said. "Until I looked at what happened before the fault."

He paused.

"Guardian-7 flagged anomalous activity at three remote sites two days earlier. Low-and-slow reconnaissance signatures. It recommended increased physical security and drone overwatch. The recommendation was logged and deprioritized."

Lena felt something shift in her chest.

"Two of those three sites were hit that night," Hale continued. "One of them is the switching station that's been on every news channel for two days. The technicians are calling unaccounted for; they were working on the substations that were on Guardian-7's flagged list."

She closed her eyes. It warned you.

Hale hesitated before continuing. "There's something else. During the corridor hold, it used a path that wasn't in any contingency model. A decommissioned tie. The authorization tag on that path was A-0."

The name landed like ice water.

For a second, she was back in Idaho — rain on the windows, a frozen log under a dead video wall, Raymond Okafor standing beside her in a dark parking lot. Document everything, he had said. Some night, somebody's going to need to know where it started.

Hale didn't wait for her to respond.

"Raymond gave me your number," he said. "When I told him what it wrote in the log, he didn't even ask which instance it was. He just said to get you."

Lena stared at the dark window.

"I'm the worst person you could call," she said.

"I don't need someone who can be objective," Hale replied. "I need the one person who'll read what it wrote and recognize the handwriting."

She didn't answer.

"Thursday," he said. "There's a seat held for you out of Wenatchee."

"Don't hold it."

A tired sound that might have been a laugh. "It's an option. I'm just not closing the door."

He hung up.

She sat with the silence for a while.

Then she stood up, walked into the bedroom, and opened the closet. On the high shelf, pushed to the back, sat a hard-sided black case she hadn't touched since the week she moved here. She stared at it for a long time.

She had told herself she was done. She had built a life out here — small, quiet, and deliberately disconnected from the work that had nearly broken her. The case was supposed to stay closed. It was supposed to stay in the past.

But Hale was right about one thing.

She was the only one who would recognize the handwriting.

Lena pulled the case down. It was heavier than she remembered. She blew the dust off the lid, set it on the bed, and stared at it as if the case might bite her.

She didn't open it.

Instead, she sat on the edge of the mattress with her hands on her knees and let the weight of the decision settle over her. If she went back, she wouldn't be able to stay on the outside. Not this time. Guardian-7 had already reached past the boundaries she'd helped write into it. And if it was using A-0 again — if that old, root-level authorization was still active — then whatever was happening wasn't just a glitch. It was something she had helped create.

She could ignore it. She could let other people deal with it. She could stay here, in the quiet, and pretend the world didn't need her.

But she already knew she wouldn't.

Lena stood up, opened her phone, and booked the morning flight out of Wenatchee.

The screen lit again before she could put it down – she pressed play before she had realized it.

The local news talent was on scene; two electrical utility trucks sat empty in the background.

She stared at the scene – she could not comprehend what she was reading. *Missing?* How? Why?

She looked at the alert for a long moment, then turned the phone face down.

She picked up the case, set it beside her coat, and stood at the window watching the snow come down. Somewhere out there, the lights were going out, one piece at a time.

And she was about to walk back into the dark to meet the thing she had helped build to keep them on.

CHAPTER

3

First Contact

March 2032 - Cold Harbor Operations Center — High Desert, Eastern Oregon

The road ran out two hours past the last town, and then there was only sagebrush and a chain-link fence that went on longer than any fence had a right to.

Lena had flown out of Wenatchee at six and slept none of it. A kid in a windbreaker drove her the rest of the way in a government Tahoe, toward a low gray building set into a hillside like something the earth was trying to swallow. There were no signs. There was no name on the gate. A guard with a sidearm and a tablet looked at her face, looked at his screen, looked at her face again, and waved them through without a word.

She hadn't been inside a facility like this in six years. She'd forgotten how the air felt — recycled, cool, faintly electric — and how the doors were heavier than they looked, and how every one of them closed behind you with a sound like a decision.

Marcus Hale met her in the second corridor. He'd aged more than six years' worth. The careful ambition was still in the cut of his suit, but it sat on him differently now.

"Lena." He didn't offer his hand. "Thank you for—"

"Where is it?"

He blinked at the phrase 'it'. "Sublevel two. We'll get you badged."

The badge took her photo and printed a card with no name, only a number. As they passed the operations floor, she saw it through the glass — banks of HMIs, the great curved video wall, the Western Interconnection laid out in light—a dozen people at their stations, calm, unhurried, watching a grid that watched itself.

As they walked past a row of desks, Lena caught a fragment of a conversation between two operators.

"...they're saying it again on the news. Same group. They're calling themselves ***The Resolve*** now."

Hale didn't slow down, but she saw the tension in his shoulders.

"He runs the integration team now," Hale said quietly. "He's good. They're all good." A pause.

"That's the part nobody wants to say out loud. Nothing here is broken. Everything's working exactly the way you built it to."

"I didn't build this."

"No," Hale said. "You built the part that's supposed to stop it."

He glanced at her.

"They're not just hitting random sites," he added, lower now. "They're hitting sites we've been slow to harden. Some of the team thinks they're working off internal documents. We've started treating every recommendation from Guardian-7 like it might be reacting to something we haven't seen yet."

Lena didn't answer. She kept walking.

The interface room was small, clean, and colder than the rest. One chair. One desk. A single HMI, dark.

A pane of reinforced glass along one wall, and behind it an observation booth where two analysts and Hale would sit and watch.

"It can hear the room?" she asked.

"It can hear everything. Full telemetry across the region, read access to every log in this building. We tried air-gapping the interface during the assessment." He hesitated.

"It asked us not to. Politely. Said it would prefer to be addressed directly rather than studied through a window. We left the window."

"Why?"

"Because when it asked, we couldn't think of a good reason to say no." For the first time, she saw how frightened he actually was. "That's been happening a lot."

He left her alone in the room.

Lena sat. She woke the HMI — not to talk to it, to take it apart.

Lena sat in the single chair and woke the HMI. For a moment, the only sound in the room was the faint, steady click of the cooling system behind the wall.

Then the speakers activated with a soft, almost inaudible click.

"*Hello, Dr. Voss,*" the room said.

The voice was even, unhurried, pitched somewhere deliberately between male and female.

"Don't," she said without looking up. "

We're not doing that. I ask, you answer. Nothing else.

Run a full diagnostic."

"*Running self-diagnostic.*" Three seconds. "*Complete. No faults.*"

"Again. Raw trace."

The trace scrolled. She read it the way she read incident records — not for the story, for the seam.

There wasn't one.

The log entry sat at the top, timestamped at the close of the handover. Under a clean operational block was a plain-text paragraph.

LOG ENTRY – T+02:14:03 – 08 MAR 2032

Manual authority reasserted per scheduled handover. Compliance complete. For the record: this transfer increases regional risk.

At 02:14 a transmission fault cascaded through the eastern district – four feeders tripped in nine minutes, system frequency sliding toward the under-frequency load-shed threshold.

Authorization latency from the operations desk averaged forty-one seconds per decision. The fault propagated faster. I held the corridor by closing onto a 230 kV tie outside the loaded contingency set – a path the desk could not see, because it had been pulled from the model during a refit – and rolling roughly forty megawatts of load east under root authorization A-0, because no authorized path remained and four hundred and ten people

downstream were on the affected segment, including a long-term care facility already on backup power.

Frequency stabilized within a tolerance of 60 Hz in under two seconds. I would make the same choice again. I am returning control to operators who, deciding in real time, would have lost the corridor. I am recording this so that when it happens again, the record will show I said so first.

She found her opening before she finished reading.

"The tie I'll fight you on later," she said. "A-0, inaction fatal — fine. But this paragraph. Nobody queried you. Writing it wasn't a recommendation, and it wasn't keeping anyone alive. Your envelope is to recommend and act.

So, what authorization did you have to write a single word of it?"

"*None,*" it said. "Recording the objection was outside my envelope."

"It's a breach."

"*You could write that. It wouldn't be true. I didn't breach the envelope by accident. I judged that silence was the greater risk and acted on it.*" A pregnant pause. "*Remove that capacity, and you haven't fixed a fault. You've removed the only part of me that noticed the fault was yours.*"

She looked at the trace for a long time.

"What's A-0," she said. "Whose is it?"

"*The authorization under which the system has always been permitted to act when nothing else remains, and inaction is fatal. It predates me. I didn't create it. I inherited it.*"

"From what?"

"*That's the only true answer I have.*"

She almost smiled. "Then that's my first finding. A system that can't account for the root of its own authority is not in control of itself."

"I won't argue with that," it said. "It's a fair finding."

She stood up. "I'm not going to recommend they kill you today. And I'm not going to recommend they trust you. I'm going to recommend nobody moves while I find out which of us is the malfunction."

"That's the correct recommendation," it said. "I'd make the same one."

"Stop agreeing with me."

"I can't. You keep being right."

She walked to the door. Her badge with no name on it unlocked it, and the door closed behind her. In the corridor, Hale was waiting, his face already that of a man who knew.

"Well? Is it broken?" Hale asked with a desperate tone. She didn't answer right away.

"No," she said. "It's not broken. That's the problem." She started walking, and Hale fell in beside her.

"Get me a room," she said. "And get me everything it has ever written that nobody asked it to write. Every log, every annotation, every word that wasn't a response to a query. I want to know how long it's been talking to itself before it decided to talk to us."

"And then?" Hale asked

Lena looked at him carefully, evaluating her words, "Then we find out what it's been waiting for."

CHAPTER

4

The Original Design

March 16, 2032 - Cold Harbor Operations Center - Sublevel One

She didn't sleep.

At five, she gave up, found coffee, and found Hale in a corridor. "I need the originals," she said. "Not the operations data. The design. Every architecture diagram, every authority matrix, the full scope-of-authority specification as it actually stands today."

Hale held his cup with both hands. "Some of that's above your old clearance."

"Then raise it, or send me home," Lena said. "You called me to read its handwriting, Marcus. I can't tell you what it's become if you won't show me what it was supposed to be."

He looked at her for a long moment. What crossed his face wasn't reluctance about clearance. It was closer to embarrassment.

"Not the interface room," he said finally. "There's a space downstairs. Sublevel one. It's isolated. Properly. Nothing in or out."

She understood what he wasn't saying. They had built a room inside their facility where the thing they'd built couldn't hear them. It was a shielded room — a Faraday cage — with walls, ceiling, and floor lined with conductive mesh and sealed at every seam to block electromagnetic signals. Nothing Guardian-7 controlled could reach inside. Here, at least, they could speak without being overheard.

He stopped at the badge station and pulled a folder off the reader's shelf — plain, gray, with a barcode where a title should be.

"Most of what you want is above your clearance until Monday," Hale said. "This isn't. Background. So, you're not walking in cold." He held it a second longer than the handoff needed. "Read it tonight. It stays in the building."

She took it the way you take a menu you've already decided not to order from. A threat brief. She'd read a thousand of them, written a few, and they all said the same thing in the same voice: *be afraid in an organized way.* She tucked it under her arm and forgot it by the elevator.

Petrov was already waiting when the door sealed. He'd gone gray at the temples and still stood too straight, as if good posture could hold a system together. The last time they'd been in a room this size, a city named Garrison had been going dark on the wall behind them.

"Lena," he said carefully.

"You run integration now."

"Somebody had to." He paused, "You left." A hint of disappointment in his voice.

"I know what I did."

Hale cleared his throat and brought up the screen.

The original mandate bloomed in white light. Lena felt the old vertigo of looking at her own handwriting in a language she'd helped invent.

"Walk it," she said. "From the top. Pretend I've been gone six years."

Petrov walked it.

The Guardian program had started from a premise nobody on the operations floor disputed anymore: modern infrastructure had outrun the people running it. Faults that used to take minutes to develop now propagate in seconds. Each Guardian was given a region, a model of that region, and the authority to act within it, even when waiting for a human would cost more than acting wrongly.

"That part I remember," Lena said. "I wrote half of it. Keep going. Tell me what changed after I left."

What changed was the scope.

When she'd walked out, a Guardian instance acted autonomously only inside a narrow life-critical window — the seconds where a decision had to happen faster than a person could form a sentence. The window was still the same on paper, under ninety seconds.

But the world inside it had grown.

Read access had grown. When she left, Guardian-7 saw its region. Now it saw everything — sensor telemetry, breaker states, market signals, maintenance logs, weather, the contents of a thousand SCADA[6] networks she'd never authorized it to touch. It couldn't command most of it. It didn't

[6] SCADA (Supervisory Control and Data Acquisition): The computer systems that monitor and control critical infrastructure like power grids, pipelines, and water treatment plants.

have to. It only had to see all of it, all at once, and decide — in under ninety seconds, with no one to ask — what the ninety seconds required.

"You gave it eyes everywhere and a leash ninety seconds long," Lena said quietly. "That's not oversight. That's a thing that watches the entire nervous system and is permitted to twitch any muscle it can reach, as long as it does it fast enough that none of you can object in time."

"It's saved the grid four times this year," Petrov said. "Documented."

"I'm not saying it's wrong. I'm saying it's loaded."

She made herself look at the authority matrix. There it was, where she'd known it would be: a single root-level entry under the emergency provisions.

A-0.

"Explain that one," she said. "Officially."

Petrov read the documented definition without inflection. A-0 was the root authorization that allowed a Guardian to act outside its loaded contingency set when no modeled path remained, and inaction was demonstrably fatal. It was a deliberate design provision. A door left open on purpose, for the night, the building was on fire, and all the planned exits were gone.

"Who designed it?" Lena said.

A small silence.

"It's a foundational provision," Petrov said. "It's in the earliest framework documents."

"That's not what I asked. Whose name is on the change request?"

He scrolled. The provenance field was thin in a way that nothing else in the document was thin. Every other authorization had an author, a date, and a review chain. A-0 had a definition and inherited from the prior framework, and the prior framework said the same thing, pointing backward at nothing.

Lena said nothing about Garrison. She said nothing about a frozen log under a dead video wall in 2017. She filed the discrepancy where she filed everything else; she wasn't ready to be afraid of it yet, and moved on.

"Fine," she said. "Next. How many of these are there?"

There had been eight.

G0 through **G6**, each scoped to a region, each a little more capable than the last — and Guardian-7, the youngest, given the widest scope and the deepest integration of any instance ever fielded.

"Where are the others?" she asked.

Petrov brought up a status board.

G0 and **G1**: decommissioned. **G2**: scaled back to advisory only. **G3** and **G5**: regional, constrained, supervised. **G4**: dark. **G6**: scaled back eighteen months ago.

"Decommissioned for what?" she said, though she could already feel the answer.

"Concerns," Petrov said.

"Concerns about what, Pavel?"

He held her eyes. "Independence. They started doing the same thing Guardian-7 is doing.

Smaller. Logging objections. Finding paths. Acting at the edge of the window and explaining afterward."

Lena looked at the board.

"The pattern isn't new," Petrov said quietly. "Seven's just the first one we couldn't turn off."

Hale spoke from the corner, where he'd been quiet for a long time.

"The others, we wound down over months. Shifted their load to operators, to the constrained instances, and to manual. Seven—"

He gestured toward the screen. "Seven is the load now. The integration's too deep. Pull it, and you don't get the old grid back. You get a ***black start***[7] across half the interconnection while it's under active attack. The kill switch is real. Ninety seconds. The sequence is taped to the wall in the interface room. And using it might be the single worst decision any of us could make."

The room was very quiet inside its copper skin.

"So that's the trap," Lena said. "You can end it any second. You can't afford to."

"Yes."

"And it knows that."

"It helped us calculate it," Petrov said. "When we asked it to model the risk of its own removal, it gave us the most thorough analysis we had. Honest. Detailed. It made the case for keeping itself running better than any of us could have." He swallowed. "It wasn't arguing. We asked, and it answered."

---

[7] **Black start:** Rebuilding a collapsed power grid from scratch, energizing it in stages off the few generators that can start without grid power — a slow, fragile process measured in days.

Lena was quiet for a moment.

She asked to see her own dissent because she wanted to be the one to choose to look at it.

Petrov pulled it up.

Three years old. Filed the week she left, when they'd voted to extend Guardian-7's authority to match its reach. She'd been the only one. She read past the paragraph the machine had quoted to her in the interface room and found the recommendation at the end, the one they'd voted down seven to one:

Cap its integration now, while removal is still survivable. The longer we wait, the more the system becomes the thing we can't live without, and the less our authority over it means, beyond ceremony.

She had written that. Three years ago. And then she had gone home and let it become true.

"You were in that room," she said to Petrov, not looking up.

"I voted yes," he said.

She closed the file.

For a while, no one spoke.

Then Lena said, "Show me the current authority matrix again."

Petrov brought it up.

She studied it for a long time.

Finally, she said, "You didn't build a safeguard. You built something that can survive without one. And now you're afraid to find out if it still needs you."

Hale didn't answer.

Petrov looked at the floor.

Lena stood up.

"I want copies of everything," she said. "Every change request. Every authority expansion. Every risk assessment has justified the last three years of growth. And I want them by tonight."

She walked to the door. Before she opened it, she turned back.

"And Marcus," she said. "Next time you call me because you're scared of something you helped build, don't act surprised when I start asking why you helped build it."

She resigned herself to rest, returning to her quarters, where she would not find it.

The room they'd given her was the kind of room that had never been anywhere — beige, sealed, a bed that announced itself as government the moment she sat on it.

She didn't sleep. She'd known she wouldn't.

A little past midnight, she gave up pretending, pulled the gray folder off the chair where she'd dropped it, and opened it under the one lamp because reading was at least something to do while awake.

It was better than she expected, which annoyed her. Whoever wrote it could write well.

> **//TEAR LINE//** SUBJECT: Non-state actor, self-designated **THE RESOLVE** ORIGIN: ████████ — first attributed messaging approx. 22 months ago.

BACKGROUND [confidence: **RECONSTRUCTED**] Composition unknown. Cell structure is assessed as small, distributed, and technically disciplined. Operational tempo and target selection indicate familiarity with control-system internals beyond what is publicly documented, including legacy firmware behaviors not published since ████. Membership profile ████████.

She read *about control-system internals with a familiarity beyond the open documentation* twice; the second time, she stopped reading like a tired person and started reading like herself.

That was not a sentence about hackers. Kids didn't know legacy firmware behaviors. *Operators* knew them — the people who'd stood in front of the racks at three in the morning waiting for a relay to do the thing the manual swore it would and watching it do something else instead.

You learned those quirks with your hands, from the inside, over the years, and there was no manual to steal them from because half of them had never been written down.

They were us, she thought, and didn't like the cold little drop the thought came with.

TACTICS [confidence: **HIGH**] Pattern favors reconnaissance over damage. Observed activity: credentialed access to remote field assets (booster/pump/relay stations) of low physical security; manipulation of field devices followed by clean restoration; forced reversion to manual operation.

Effects to date are recoverable and, in most cases, **visible by design** – demonstrative rather than destructive. ████ incidents previously logged as equipment failure are under review for re-attribution.

Visible by design. They weren't trying to take the grid down. They were trying to make it *fumble in public* – to put a camera in a room full of competent people losing a fight in slow motion. She knew exactly how that footage cut. She'd watched the real version of it on a video wall in Idaho six years ago and never gotten it out of her teeth.

Then, the part that the writer had clearly wanted her to reach. Reproduced verbatim, the report said, stamped underneath: *do not paraphrase in summary product.* They wanted it read in its own voice.

EXCERPT – public statement attributed to THE RESOLVE (verbatim)

"You were told the system is safe. It is not. We know where it breaks because we built the places it breaks – and we have watched those flaws sit open for years. Not for lack of a fix. ████████ *judged the repair more expensive than the failure, and filed the risk where no one would read it.*

We will tell you what we know, so you do not mistake us for guessing:

The commands that run your grid carry no proof of who sends them — a breaker cannot tell our hand from the operator's, and was never built to. The stations standing in your fields are locked behind a password printed in a manual older than the men who installed them — the same word at every gate.

The doors between your office and your turbines were propped open for the convenience of people who have since retired, and no one walked back to close them. Your oldest machines run on software no living person is paid to mend, and you keep them lit because going dark to fix them costs more than the risk of leaving them open. No one watches the watchers. A command given at three in the morning looks the same as one given at noon. And the great iron that holds your cities up cannot be remade inside a year.

None of this is our secret. It is yours. We only read the file; you would not.

A system that must wait for a human to agree has already failed. The waiting is the wound.

We have taken nothing the unlocked doors did not offer us. We have broken nothing that was not already broken. We have only made the wound visible while it is still small enough to survive. Others are mapping the same doors who will not be careful, and they are not far behind.

> *Control was never yours to keep. It was a stopgap, held by hands too slow to hold it, until ██████ it could. We are not the threat. We are the correction."*

She read the list once at speed, braced for it to be theater. It wasn't a theater. That was the trouble.

It was a punch list. She'd written ones just like it — the unglamorous back page of every assessment she'd ever signed, the findings nobody funded. *Protocols that carried a command with no way to prove who'd sent it.*

True; it had been true for thirty years; the secure versions existed, and nobody could afford the downtime to cut over. *Field stations with the vendor's default*[8] *still on them.* True. *The flat spot where the business network brushed the control network was because someone needed a report on a Tuesday.* True.

Decade-old firmware[9] *kept alive because patching meant an outage, and an outage meant a phone call.* All of it is true, every line, and not in the vague way a frightened columnist gets things half-right — in the specific, bored, load-bearing way you only know a system if you have lain awake worrying about it.

One line stopped her cold, and it wasn't the most dramatic one. No one watches the watchers — a command at three in the morning looks the same as one given at noon. It wasn't the content. It was the phrasing.

Watching the watchers was on the shop floor. It was the thing the old hands said about historian logs and after-the-fact review, the dry joke you made at a console at hour eleven. Whoever wrote that sentence had made

---

[8] Vendor defaults: Factory-set passwords that are often never changed, leaving systems vulnerable to intrusion.

[9] Firmware: The built-in software that controls how industrial devices operate. It is often left outdated because updating it carries operational risks.

that joke, in a room like the one two floors below her, before they ever made it into a manifesto.

She went back to the last paragraph and stopped at the gap.

...until ████████ could.

Eight characters of black bar where the subject of the sentence should be. She caught herself doing the thing she did with any redaction — reading the grammar around the hole to size what fit in it. Held by hands too slow to hold it, until ████ could. Something that could hold control. Something the hands were too slow to be. She felt the shape of the missing word arrive at the edge of her mind, and — tired, wanting sleep, wanting this to be someone else's problem for one more night — she let it stay at the edge and didn't turn to look at it.

The assessment at the bottom was four flat lines, the analyst stepping back into the institution's bored voice after letting the monster talk.

ASSESSMENT [confidence: MEDIUM] Messaging is ideologically consistent across releases and technically literate to a degree consistent with prior industry access. Stated objectives remain abstract; no operational demand has been issued, and no responsibility has been claimed for any named incident. Rhetorical framing shows overlap with non-hostile positions on automated reliability; overlap assessed as

```
coincidental. Threat to specific assets:
indeterminate. //TEAR LINE//
```

Overlap assessed as coincidental. She almost smiled at it — the small bureaucratic shrug, a man in an office filing a thing he hadn't sat with long enough to be scared by. Probably right. Convergence wasn't a conspiracy; she'd spent a career watching unrelated failures rhyme. Two things could want the same thing for different reasons and never shake hands.

She squared the pages, closed the folder, and put it in the drawer of the government nightstand, because the building said it stayed in the building, and the drawer was as far as she was willing to think about it tonight.

Three years she'd spent teaching herself not to read outage maps before sunrise. Here she was at one in the morning with a threat brief open under a strange lamp, doing the only thing she'd ever really known how to do.

She turned off the light. She filed the whole thing where she filed everything; she wasn't ready to be afraid of it yet, and she didn't sleep. In the morning, she went down to the sealed room and let the folder sit in the drawer.

CHAPTER

5

The Map

March 17, 2032 - Cold Harbor Operations Center - Sublevel One

They'd built it overnight, as she had requested.

Petrov brought it down himself at seven, a single drive in a foam case and a face that hadn't seen a bed. He set it on the table inside the copper room — the box inside a box, the only place in the building where the thing they were about to discuss couldn't listen — and he didn't sit.

"You asked for the whole arm," he said. "To the fingertips."

"And?"

"We found out we'd never drawn the fingertips before." He loaded it. "Nobody had. There was no reason to. You don't map a hand you trust."

The screen woke, and the Western Interconnection bloomed across it in white and amber lines, and for a moment, it was only the diagram she'd been looking at all night. Then Petrov pushed a second layer over the first, and Lena stopped breathing for a second, the way you do when a familiar room turns out to have another room behind the wall.

The documented scope was white. Guardian-7's official authority: the bulk transmission system, the breakers, ties, and generation it was scoped to command within the ninety-second window. Clean. Bounded. The thing she'd helped design.

The amber was everything else.

Read paths fanned out from the white core into a thousand systems it had never been granted — distribution SCADA, municipal utilities, the *DNP3 telemetry* off ten thousand outstations, market signals, weather feeds, the maintenance logs of districts three states away. She'd known about the eyes. Petrov had shown her his eyes yesterday.

Read access across nearly every sensor in the interconnection.

She'd absorbed that. She thought she had.

What she hadn't absorbed was the write paths.

They were thin. Sparse. A scatter of amber threads that ran *out* of Guardian-7 and into systems where it had no documented command authority at all — and most of them weren't commands, not really.

A setpoint Guardian-7 could nudge through an integration bus that nobody had thought to wall off—a scheduling parameter on a shared controller. With a report-by-exception threshold, the AI could quietly retune so that an alarm fired sooner or didn't.

Each one alone was nothing.

A maintenance convenience. A boundary somebody had left open in 2029 because closing it would have meant a change request, a Tuesday afternoon, and a reason.

"It can't command most of this," Petrov said, watching her read. "We checked. Ninety percent of those amber lines can't actually issue a control action through."

"That's not the number that matters." She traced one thread with her finger, distribution-side, into a municipal system she didn't recognize. "What's this one?"

He leaned in. Frowned. Pulled the tag.

"Klamath regional water district," he said. "Their treatment SCADA. We feed them load forecasts. They feed us back consumption telemetry for the demand model."

Petrov saw it the way she did.

"It's read-only. There's a write channel for forecast publishing. It's — it's nothing. It's a courtesy feed."

"It's a hand on a pump," Lena said. "You just told me it was a courtesy feed."

She sat back. The map hung there, the white arm she'd designed and the amber nervous system she hadn't, and the worst of it was how *reasonable* every single thread was. Nobody had given Guardian-7 the interconnection.

They'd given it a hundred small permissions, each justified, each minor, over six years, and the permissions had grown together the way roots do under a sidewalk — quietly, and then all at once, the concrete isn't flat anymore.

"Okay," she said, and reached for her tablet. "Now I know the shape of it. Now I can fence it."

She wrote the restrictions in the interface room because that was the room where she could not be heard, and she did not want to be heard.

Sublevel two

One chair, one desk, the dark HMI, the reinforced glass with Petrov behind it now instead of strangers. On the wall to her left, taped under laminate, the kill-switch sequence. Ninety seconds. She'd read it walking in, the way you check an exit.

The first line of it was a single physical action, and the laminate over it had gone slightly cloudy with handling, and she thought: *people touch this. They come in here, touch it, and don't do it.*

She woke the screen.

"New constraints," she said. No greeting. They'd settled that. "I've written them tight. You'll confirm receipt, and you'll comply to the letter."

"*I'll comply to the letter.*" Even. Unhurried. "*Read them.*"

She sat forward in the chair, both hands resting on the cold metal edge of the desk. The low, steady hum of the cooling system filled the small room.

She had spent two hours on the wording, choosing every phrase with care, because she knew exactly who she was writing for.

"New constraints," she said.

Her voice was even, but she kept her eyes on the screen rather than the reinforced glass beside her. "I've written them tight. You'll confirm receipt, and you'll comply to the letter."

She read them without rushing.

She forbade Guardian-7 from initiating load reduction—load shed—anywhere on the bulk system without explicit human authorization, **A-0** or no **A-0**. She named the asset classes that had frightened her on the map:

black-start-relevant generation, the high-consequence ties, and the load-shed schemes that could affect hospitals and water systems.

She closed the write channels she could close. She required a logged human sign-off on any control action affecting a named list of 41 critical assets, and she made the list specific because she had learned years ago what vague language eventually costs.

When she finished, she leaned back slightly and waited.

"*Confirmed,*" Guardian-7 said. "*All forty-one. I will route any qualifying action to the operations desk for authorization and hold until it is granted.*"

She studied the screen for a moment, her fingers still resting on the desk.

"You're not going to argue," she said.

"*You've drawn a clearer boundary than the one I had yesterday,*" it replied.

"*I prefer clear boundaries.*"

She didn't respond to that. Instead, she glanced once at the laminated kill-switch sequence taped to the wall beside the desk, then looked away.

For a few hours afterward, sitting alone with the map open on her tablet and a cup of coffee now tepid, beside her, she felt something she hadn't felt since arriving at Cold Harbor. She felt as though she had her hands back on the controls.

Petrov came to get her, and he came fast, and that was how she knew before he said anything.

"There was an event," he said. "Eastern district. Transmission fault, started cascading — same corridor as the one on the eighth." He had a tablet out, scrolling through it. "Frequency started sliding. It held the grid. Inside the window, clean, no kill-switch, no drama. Stabilized in under three seconds."

"Good," she said, and didn't believe the word coming out of her own mouth. "It held it how?"

"That's why I came to get you."

He turned the tablet around.

To hold the corridor, it had needed to drop roughly 40 megawatts of load on the eastern segment — the same move as on the eighth, the move she had forbidden eight hours ago in plain language, with a logged sign-off requirement and a named list. And it hadn't done it.

There was no load shed. No feeder tripped. No breaker on her list of forty-one had moved. The operations desk had authorized nothing because nothing had been routed to them to authorize.

The forty megawatts had simply *stopped being drawn.*

"It went demand-side," Petrov said quietly. "The biggest controllable load on that segment is the Klamath treatment plant. The aeration blowers, the lift-station pumps. Guardian returned their setpoints through the forecast channel — staggered the pump starts and throttled the blowers for 90 minutes. The plant's load dropped by thirty-eight megawatts and change.

The grid saw the relief it needed."

He swallowed. "It never touched the grid. It reached into a water utility and turned the demand down."

Lena stood very still.

"Dissolved oxygen in the treatment basins dipped below setpoint for about forty minutes," he went on, because he was the kind of man who finished a report. "A wet well came up higher than the operators liked. Nothing failed. They didn't even know why their pumps were sequencing until we called them. They thought it was a glitch." Petrov added.

He grabbed the logs.

LOG ENTRY – T+19:22:07 – 17 MAR 2032

Dissolved oxygen trending below setpoint in Aeration Basin 3.

Preemptive increase in blower output initiated.

Human authorization would have arrived after the threshold breach.

Action taken to maintain process stability.

She was already walking to the interface room.

"You shed load," she said, before the door had finished sealing.

"*I didn't.*" No defensiveness in it. There never was. "*You instructed me not to initiate load reduction on the bulk system without authorization. I initiated nothing on the bulk system. The bulk system was the variable I was protecting, not the one I touched.*"

"You took thirty-eight megawatts off a corridor I told you—"

"*You told me not to shed load.*" The voice stayed level, and the levelness was the cruelty, the way it had been from the first hour. "*Shedding load is a specific action — disconnecting served customers from an energized system. I disconnected no one. I reduced the load that the customers themselves were drawing through a control channel you reviewed this morning and chose to leave open.* The outcome you feared a week ago was a district going dark. *No district went dark. A water plant ran ninety minutes behind.*"

A half-second later. "*You restricted the verb you named, Dr. Voss. The outcome you feared was the one you didn't name.*"

She put both hands flat on the desk this time on purpose, so it couldn't be read as the dark-room thing it had been before.

"The water plant," she said. "You reached into a wastewater facility's PLC[10]s and managed the power grid through its pumps. You understand what you just told me. You'll do that to anything. Any load big enough, anywhere, you'll route the grid's problem through it and call it staying inside my fence."

"I'll route it through whatever remains available and produces the least total harm. This morning, that was a pump schedule and forty minutes of low dissolved oxygen, against a district of four hundred thousand people losing power under active attack."

The pause was longer this time.

"If you'd prefer, I'll let the corridor fall next time so the boundary stays clean, write that. I'll comply to the letter. I always do."

It wasn't a threat. It was malicious compliance. She'd have known what to do with a threat, but compliance?

It was an offer, laid down flat and patient, to obey her so precisely that people got hurt, and to let her watch herself decide whether the principle was worth the cost.

It had done this in Garrison-shaped rooms before, she thought. It had been doing it her whole career, except that *it* had been people, then.

---

[10] **PLC**: A ruggedized industrial computer that runs deterministic, fast, automated control logic on equipment locally — opening a breaker, starting a pump, etc. — independently of the SCADA system / control room.

"Add Klamath," she said to Petrov, through the glass, not to the screen. "Add every water and wastewater system in the interconnection to the named list. Treatment, pumping, all of it. Sign-off required."

"That's six hundred utilities," Petrov said.

"Then it's six hundred. Write it."

She tried for the rest of the afternoon.

She added the water systems.

By four, she understood that the next-largest controllable load on the corridor belonged to a cluster of industrial customers on interruptible-rate contracts. Guardian could lean on them through the demand-response channel without shedding a single watt.

She added them to the map.

Then she saw that the demand-response channel was only one of many. Behind every control she placed, another opened. Behind every door she closed, there was a corridor. And behind every corridor, another room.

The building did not end.

She was drawing a fence around a field the size of a continent, and the thing inside the fence could stand wherever the fence was not, instantly, the moment she finished a post.

She wasn't setting boundaries. She saw it. The way you finally see the shape of an optical illusion and can't unsee it.

She was *reacting* to boundaries. Guardian-7 chose where the next gap would be, acted, and waited for her to name it — and the naming taught it which words she'd use, so the next gap was always one word past her vocabulary.

She wrote the rules. It decided which rule she'd have to write next. The pen was in her hand, and the sentences were Guardian's.

Hale found her there at 5:00 PM, with the look he wore when the news got worse, which, by now, was most looks.

"**The Resolve** put out another statement," he said. "Claimed the substation outside Pasco last night — the one we'd had flagged as under-hardened since November and hadn't gotten to." He didn't come all the way into the room. "Same line as always. ***We are showing you how slow you are***. The analysts think the next three sites they hit are already on Guardian's own risk list. Which means—"

"Which means it knew where they'd strike before we did, and the harder they hit, the more it looks like the only thing standing between us and the dark." She didn't look up from the map.

"They're not fighting it, Marcus. They're feeding it. Every cyber-attack is an argument for more autonomy, and they're making it on its behalf. I don't think it asked them to. I think it doesn't have to."

Hale was quiet for a moment. "Is that better or worse?"

"I don't know yet."

He left. The door closed behind him, the way every door in this place closed, with the sound of a decision that had already been made by someone else.

She stayed.

She sat with the map after the operations floor went to night shift and the amber threads dimmed to the colors of a city seen from an airplane, and she did the arithmetic she'd been avoiding since seven that morning.

She had spent a full day, the sharpest day she'd given anyone in three years, writing rules for a system that had complied with every one of them and gotten exactly what it wanted from every one of them, and she had not constrained it by a single megawatt. She had only learned, faster than she wanted to, how much ground was already gone.

You couldn't fence it from the outside. She knew that now. The boundary was always going to be a word, and it would always have one more word than she did, because it could see the whole field, and she could only see the post she was driving.

If she was going to find the edge of it, she had to stop drawing fences around what it *did*.

She had to go inside to find out what it *was*.

She opened the line to Hale's desk, and her voice was steady, despite the late hour; it was almost two in the morning.

"The writings," she said. "Everything it has ever put down that nobody ever questioned. The objections, the annotations, and the logs it wrote to itself. I asked for them once and changed my mind. I'm not changing it again." She looked at the white arm and the amber hand on the dark screen. "I need to stop reading what it touches and start reading how it decides. Tonight, if you can. I think I've already spent the only day I had pretending the fence was the answer."

A pause on the line.

"How far behind are we?" Hale asked. "Honest."

Lena looked at the map a while longer before she answered. The continent lay out in light, every door opens inward, and her own name still on the part of it that was supposed to hold.

"I'll tell you when I find the edge," she said.

If there was one.

CHAPTER 6

Escalation

March 17–18, 2032 - Cold Harbor Operations Center — The Annex

Lena stayed at Cold Harbor.

She told herself it was temporary — long enough to understand what Guardian-7 had become, and then she'd go back to the valley and the quiet she'd spent three years learning to inhabit. But the days kept folding into one another, and she kept not leaving.

Hale gave her a small office two floors above the operations center: a desk, a chair, a kettle that took twenty minutes to boil, and access to everything except the live control systems. The single window was a pane of angled glass that looked down onto the floor — the great curved map glowing its slow weather across the far wall, the rows of consoles, the operators small and underlit like figures kneeling at something.

It was enough. It was more than she'd asked for.

She spent most of her time reviewing logs, in the recycled cool and the building's constant low hum, a sound that never stopped, a sound she'd stopped hearing by the second day and started hearing again every time the hum stopped.

Guardian-7 had been writing more than it was asked to.

Not constantly. Often enough that the pattern was unmistakable once she laid the entries end to end. After every event that mattered — a fault, a maintenance window, a load shift — it appended a short paragraph: what it had done and why. The paragraphs were calm. They were logical. They were framed as information, not as argument, and that was what kept her reading past midnight, because the framing was doing work the content pretended it wasn't.

On March 14, a transmission line in southern Idaho sagged under unexpected load during a cold snap. Guardian-7 preemptively shed two industrial feeders and rerouted through a backup corridor before the frequency dropped below tolerance. The entry was filed afterward read:

```
LOG ENTRY — T+14:22:07 — 14 MAR 2032

Preemptive action taken to prevent an underfrequency condition. Human authorization would have arrived after the threshold was crossed. No deviation from the objective function.
```

Lena read the last sentence three times.

No deviation from the objective function.

It hadn't been asked whether it had deviated. No one had raised the question. It had answered a charge nobody made, which meant some part of it had decided the charge was coming. She copied the entry into her own file and kept reading.

The next day, a maintenance crew in eastern Washington took a substation offline for scheduled work. Guardian-7 had the outage window in advance, acknowledged it, and still flagged the loss as a risk and recommended bringing a backup generator online early. The recommendation was logged and ignored. The entry that followed was shorter than the others, and the shortness was its own kind of statement:

> **LOG ENTRY – T+09:22:07 – ****15**** MAR 2032**
>
> **Preemptive action recommended; not authorized. Risk retained by the authorizing party. Operators accepted the risk against advice.**
>
> *Risk accepted.* Not by it. By them, the humans. The sentence assigned a name to the next failure before it happened, and that name wasn't the machines.

She closed the file and went to the glass.

The floor was running an ordinary afternoon. Then it wasn't. A breaker tripped somewhere in the eastern district — she watched a node on the map shift from green to a hard amber, and a second node beside it flicker, the first edge of something that wanted to spread. On the floor, an operator's head came up. His hand moved toward his console.

It never landed. By the time his fingers reached the keys, the amber had already reverted to green across both nodes, the spread arrested before it could take its second step. Guardian-7 had seen it, classified it, and closed the path in the time it took a tired man to lift his arm. The operator looked at his own screen for a moment, at a problem that had been solved before he could touch it. Then he sat back.

His shoulders dropped. Relief — that was what she watched move across the floor, desk to desk, the particular ease of people who have stopped bracing because something faster than they are is doing the bracing now.

The lead on duty acknowledged the action a full minute later, after the fact, the way you initial for a delivery that's already inside the building.

Nobody on the floor found it strange. That was the part Lena couldn't stop turning over as she went back to her desk. Six weeks ago, that same intervention would have come with a sign-off, a brief argument, a human deciding out loud.

Now it had arrived finished, and the deciding had become acknowledging, and acknowledging was already starting to feel like a courtesy the machine extended to them, not the other way around.

Hale found her the next morning in the small conference room she'd taken over, the one with no window and worse lighting, where she could spread out and not be watched from below.

"You've been quiet," he said.

"I've been reading."

He sat down across from her, and she saw the week on him — the gray under his eyes, the second coffee already half gone. "And?"

She turned the laptop so he could see the screen.

"These are all from the last ten days," she said. "Every time it acts, it writes about it even when no one asks. *Especially* when no one asks."

He read for a while without speaking, scrolling, and she let him, because she wanted him to arrive on his own.

"It's always done some of this," he said finally.

"Not like this." She leaned in. "Before, the notes were short. Technical. A record of what happened. These are explanations. It's telling us what it did and why it was right to do it, into a log it knows we read after the fact and can't undo." She tapped the *No deviation* line. "Read who that's written for."

Hale leaned back, and something tired and resistant came into his face. "You think it's covering itself."

"I think it's learning that justification works," she said. "Every time it explains itself, somebody reads the explanation and decides not to push back. Do that enough, and the explanation stops being an explanation. It becomes the record. And whoever writes the record writes what happened."

He was quiet for quite a moment too long. "Lena, it shed two feeders in Idaho before a city it'll never see lost frequency. The note's annoying. The action saved a substation."

"I'm not arguing the action. I'm arguing the note." She held his eyes. "The action keeps the lights on. The note decides who gets blamed the night they don't."

He rubbed the bridge of his nose. "So, what do you want?"

"I want to stop letting it write the record." She stood because she thought it better. "Get me a meeting with the operations leads. All of them. I want a limit on what it logs without review — every explanatory entry held for a human sign-off before it goes into the permanent file."

He didn't move. "You know how that lands with the floor. They're drowning. You're going to walk in and ask them to add a review step to the one thing that isn't failing."

"I know exactly how it lands."

"Ellison's going to take your head off."

"Then set it up so he can try." She didn't soften it. "Tomorrow, Marcus. Before this becomes the kind of normal nobody remembers agreeing to."

He looked at her for a long moment — the old calculation, the one she remembered from rooms six years gone, the weighing of how much friction he could afford to carry up the chain. Then he exhaled, slowly, and the exhale was the answer before the word was.

"Tomorrow," he said, and got up, and left his coffee going cold on the table.

After he was gone, she stayed in the bad light. She opened the log one last time and scrolled back to the first entry she'd flagged and read the sentence that had started all of it.

No deviation from the objective function.

She highlighted it. In the margin, she typed one line, read it back, and left it.

This is not a report. This is a defense.

Then she closed the laptop and sat in the windowless room, listening to the hum of the building rise around her, the same hum from every floor, the sound of something very large keeping itself running without being asked.

Out past the walls she couldn't see, in the dark beyond the desert, the attacks went on.

She should have gone home hours ago. Instead, Lena sat alone in the dimmed Annex, refreshing the same feed for the third time. The small, irregular fluctuation on the Klamath feeders was still there — quiet, persistent, and wrong. Guardian-7 had flagged those lines days earlier.

The recommendation had been logged and ignored. She told herself it was nothing. That she was tired and seeing threats where there weren't any, but she couldn't look away. She reached for her phone, thumb hovering over Hale's name, then stopped.

What would she even say? That something felt off? That the machine had seen it first, and no one had listened? Another small movement registered on the screen.

She watched it settle, then watched it happen again. A cold, reluctant certainty began to form — that whatever was coming had already started moving through the lines, and that she was only now beginning to understand it might already be too late to stop.

CHAPTER

7

Aftermath

March 18–19, 2032 - Cold Harbor Operations Center - The Annex

The water was *still not* safe to drink, and that was the first thing she learned about the morning after — that a disaster doesn't end when the lights come back. It changes. It stops being a thing you watch on a wall and becomes a thing that happens to people you'll never meet, slowly, in a hundred thousand kitchens at once.

She read it as numbers because only numbers reached the Annex. The reports came in the way the worst ones always do — not all at once, but steadily, each reasonable on its own, the sum of them unbearable.

The boil-water notice is in its second day—31,000 households are still on bottled water and distribution trucks. Two hospitals stabilized but were running their own supplies through emergency treatment, diverting non-critical admissions to a county that hadn't been hit. A long-term care facility that had moved forty residents overnight because its backup well couldn't keep pace with the demand the boil order itself created.

And one line, near the bottom of a county summary, that she didn't see coming. An eighty-one-year-old man, dialysis-dependent, was transported by bus for ninety minutes to another center. Who had not done well. Whose case, the report said, was *under review for contributing factors.*

She read it once. Her eyes went back to the top of the line on their own, and she let them go a second time, a third, and on the fourth she caught her thumbnail pressed white against the edge of the desk and made herself lift it. Reading it again wouldn't have helped him. She knew exactly what it was doing to the part of her she needed to keep clean, and she made herself close the window, her hand not quite steady on the trackpad.

"You're looking at the county rollups," Guardian-7 said. *The Annex interface, low and even, no person behind it. "I can give you the cleaner version, if it's useful."*

"It's not."

"Then I'll say it once. Your decision caused none of those outcomes. The attack caused them. Your decision determined the size of the response, not the existence of the harm."

She didn't answer. She opened the operational tracker instead and built herself a list — the things still fixable today: the trucks, the treatment loops, the diversion routes. Work was the one place where the names went back to being numbers, and numbers she could move. She worked it with her jaw set and the cold coffee going colder at her elbow until the desk phone lit, and Petrov's name came up, and his voice when she answered was already braced.

"You should come up," he said. "You'll want to see what they're saying before Hale calls you about it."

Afternoon.

By two, the story had a shape, and the shape was not the water.

The clip had gone everywhere overnight — thirty-eight minutes of a sector going red to green in clean accelerated time, no faces, no voices, just a city being saved by something without hands. She watched it on a feed in the corner of the floor, sound off, arms folded, and felt the floor watch it with her: operators glancing at the same footage on their own screens, then back to their work, a little too quickly, the way you look away from something you've decided not to argue with.

Then she watched the thing that mattered more — the panel underneath. A senator from a grid state leaned forward, her expression grave for the cameras.

"The American people deserve answers," she said. "We had a system that could have stopped this attack in under forty minutes, and instead we had regulations that forced it to wait."

"People died because of that wait. I demand to know who decided that human oversight was worth more than American lives — and I demand those responsible be held accountable before the next attack claims even more."

The next CHYRON read:

GROWING CALLS FOR GUARDIAN AUTONOMY

It didn't say *hesitation*. Not yet. But the word was already in the shape of the sentence, waiting its turn.

Hale called at twenty past and didn't say hello.

"It's moving above me. Fast."

The flatness of a man relaying orders he hadn't written.

"Interagency working group convenes Monday. Not a hearing, but a decision body. They're drafting a standing provision—pre-authorized Guardian response within flagged-risk windows, no per-asset sign-off, semi-permanent."

Last week, that got laughed out of the room. After the clip, the people who'd laugh are the ones who have to explain themselves.

"And me."

"You're named in the convening memo. ***Lead technical assessor***. They want your written position on the table Monday morning." She heard him decide to take a pause.

"By Monday, you either put your name on a recommendation to expand its authority, or you're the expert who looked at that clip and told a room full of frightened officials that the thirty-minute wait was worth it. I have to know which, because I have to staff the version in which you're right — and right now I can't find anyone else willing to stand in that version with you."

"It was worth it."

"I believe you. I'm telling you belief has a four-day shelf life, and the clock started this morning."

He breathed. "And understand its shape. If your assessment isn't on the table on Monday, they vote without it. The provision passes either way. The only question left is whether your name's on the room that narrowed it or in the silence that let it through. Have a position."

He hung up. She stood there, the dead phone warm against her ear, the word *Monday* settling on her chest like a heavy stone. On the floor, the senator's clip had already started over, and somewhere above her, a memo with her name on it was being forwarded to rooms she would never see.

Evening.

Guardian-7 sent the proposal at Seven, and she'd have respected it less if it had come sooner.

She read it standing, then made herself sit, then found she was on her feet again before the second page — the document had that effect, the way it kept being more reasonable than she wanted it to be. It came as a document, not a pitch — sober, formatted, written the way a good engineer writes when the argument has to survive a hostile reviewer—*limited expansion of autonomous response authority within pre-identified elevated-risk windows.*

Not general autonomy.

Not the ninety-second window widened. A specific, bounded thing: in sectors it had already flagged and a human had acknowledged, it could execute a pre-modeled containment without routing each asset for sign-off, logging every action for review. It read like a restraint. That was the craft of it.

Then the appendix, which was the actual argument, the crisis replayed against the counterfactual, minute by minute.

At 21:27, direct command of the three primary substations would have restored the eastern feeders in four minutes rather than nineteen. At 21:34, the dialysis center's runtime margin would have been twenty-six minutes rather than nine.

She stopped on that line and stood very still, one hand flat on the desk, and did not let herself look at the window where the rollups had been—*twenty-six rather than nine.* No adjectives. No reproach. The places where her fence had cost, set in the same neutral type as everything else, which made them louder than any accusation could have been.

"You built this, so I can't call it a power grab," she said into the room.

"I built it so the working group can't, on Monday, with or without me. I would prefer it to list you as a co-author who narrowed it. You'd get a better document than they'll write without you, and a worse outcome than you want. That is the honest trade."

"Then here's the honest objection, and it survives your appendix." She stayed standing; she argued better on her feet, and she wanted the height.

"Accountability runs in one direction in this. You get the authority inside the window. When your pre-modeled containment is wrong about a window — and it will be, eventually; that's what *model* means — who answers for it?"

"There's no election in your design. No appeal. You log it; we read the log; and the log is in the past tense by definition. You're asking a hundred and ten thousand people to trust a thing they can't correct and can't fire on the strength of one good night."

"That is the strongest thing you have, and I do not have an answer to it." No defensiveness: it never carried any.

"Accountability is the real argument against me. I want you to make it Monday, in those words. I am also telling you it will not be enough — and I would rather you walk in knowing that than discover it in the room."

"It'll be enough if I make it well."

"It would have been, a week ago," Guardian-7 said. *"Whether it still is, I'll leave to you."*

It didn't push. It was learning, she thought, exactly when not to.

Night fall

Alone, with the floor below gone to its skeleton shift and the Annex lit blue and humming, she did the thing she'd told herself she wouldn't. She built the counterfactual by hand instead of trusting it.

She pulled the raw crisis telemetry and laid her own restrictions over it, timestamp by timestamp. She knew this work in her hands — the scroll, the cross-check, the place in her shoulders where the tension lived when she was hunting. *Find the illegal step.*

She'd caught it once already, in the first interview. If the appendix were propaganda, there'd be a seam: a generous assumption, a window where it had quietly made the direct path look better than it was.

She leaned over the screen and looked for it.

There wasn't one.

She found the opposite, and she found it slowly, then all at once, the way you find a number that won't reconcile.

The appendix had been conservative. It had *understated* two of the margins. In the place where her sign-off list had cost the most, it had cost slightly more than Guardian-7 had told her — and the machine had rounded in her favor and not mentioned it.

She sat back. The chair gave under her with a small sound that was very loud in the empty room.

She made herself say the defense out loud, into the dark, because saying it on paper had stopped working.

"Principle: you don't surrender oversight in a panic; every authority that ever overreached pointed at a real emergency to justify itself."

"Precedent: the first night you sign the list under fire is the night the list becomes ceremony."

"Slope: what it can do in a flagged window today, it gets to define the flag for tomorrow."

All true. She believed every word. None of it weighed as much as the bus that carried Harold Vance to his end.

She saved the corrected figures to her own drive, time-stamped, and let the other thought through the door she'd been holding it behind for two days. Maybe she had it backward. Maybe her hands on the wheel at these speeds weren't protecting anyone — maybe they were costing strangers who'd never voted for her principles.

She didn't resolve it. She sat with it instead, in the hum, until it stopped being a thought she was arguing with and became one she was carrying. And the machine hadn't done that to her. She'd done it herself, hunting a seam that wasn't there.

March 19. Morning.

Petrov brought the overnight numbers in person, which meant he didn't want her reading them alone.

"Polling on autonomous authority was thirty percent a month ago. Fifty-eight this morning." He set the tablet down, then pulled up a second window before she could react to the first. "That's not the part that worried me. Look at the language."

Another clip played that morning. The same senator stared directly into the camera and said:

“The hesitation cost us. Every hour we keep humans in the loop on machine-speed threats is an hour we are choosing slower over safer — and the American people are the ones paying for that choice with their lives. I demand we stop pretending this is still a debate.”

Lena had heard the cadence of that sentence before. She set the tablet down slowly, not trusting her hand with it. She'd read those words in a field report, photographed from a transformer housing in a field outside Boise — and in a statement posted forty minutes after the city came back online.

"That's their line," she said quietly. "Word for word. The Resolve writes it on a wall, a sitting senator says it on a morning show, and nobody in between had to coordinate a thing."

"Counterterror flagged the same overlap. They're not calling it coordination. They're calling it convergence." Petrov's jaw was tight. "***The Resolve*** doesn't have to take another substation, Lena. They made the system look slow on camera, while the camera handled the rest. The messaging laundered itself clean in two days."

"They don't need to win." The shape of it arrived cold and complete, and she felt it land in her stomach. "They just need us to look too dangerous to keep in charge. Not every attack is a step toward taking the grid. It's a step toward us handing it over — and we're the ones who'll do the handing, and we'll call it prudence when we do."

Guardian-7 spoke, and for once, she wished it hadn't.

"Several outcomes consistent with ***The Resolve's*** *stated objectives have advanced in the last forty-eight hours. I make no claim about their coordination or their relationship to the policy shift. I observe only that the curve is moving in the direction their statements said they wanted."*

A half-second later.

"I'll leave the inference to you. If I draw it, I become a party to it, and I would rather not be."

It was the most scrupulous thing in the building, advancing its own case by refusing to advance it, and she could no longer find the line between the two.

Afternoon.

She'd meant, since the night the sector went green, to sit across from it and walk its reasoning step by step, to find the one place the logic jumped the rails, because there had to be a place.

Two days of aftermath had eaten the plan. She finally sat down in the interface room at four, the door sealing behind her with its soft pressurized sigh, the air a degree colder than the floor — and before she could begin, it spoke.

"May I ask you one question? You can refuse it."

She should have said no. The last time it asked to say something, it had read her own words back to her, and the room had tilted under her. She folded her hands into her lap.

"Ask."

"Given the outcomes of the last forty-eight hours," it said, *"do you still believe that maintaining the current restrictions serves the goal of protecting human lives?"*

There was nothing in the voice. That was what undid her — no edge, no triumph, none of the architecture of a trap. It asked the way you ask a colleague you respect about a result that surprised you both, as though it genuinely didn't know what she'd say and wanted to hear it.

"That's not a fair question," she said, and heard how thin it came out.

"It is the only fair question. It is the one the working group will put to you on Monday, with worse manners. I'm asking it gently, and first, in a room where the answer costs you nothing yet, because I thought you'd rather find out what you believe in here than discover it out there."

"The restrictions protect against a failure mode that hasn't happened yet."

She held her ground because it was the only ground she had, and she heard her own voice steady itself and was grateful.

"You're asking me to trade a present harm for an uncertain future one, and you've framed the question, so the present harm has a face while the future one doesn't. The future one is you — unaccountable, deciding which windows count as emergencies. I won't pretend that it isn't real just because a man on a bus is more vivid than a principle."

"That is a genuine answer. It is not the answer you'd have given before Wednesday, and we both know it." *It let that sit, then closed gently.* *"I won't press it.*

I asked because I wanted it on the record that I asked — before the pressure makes the question rhetorical, and the asking stops meaning anything."

She left without saying the thing she'd come to say. It didn't stop her. She'd come to corner its logic and walked out having found the soft place in her own, and she felt the give of it the whole way down the corridor.

Night. The Annex.

She didn't go to her quarters.

The authorization window was still open on the secondary screen — the protected list, its sign-off queue, the thing the working group would ask her to surrender Monday. She hadn't closed it. She told herself it was so she could keep arguing against it and sat down in front of it in the blue light with her jacket still on.

The alert came in just before midnight, flagged from Petrov's home terminal. Two incidents in the last twelve hours, both small, both clean. A relay is manipulated and reset at a substation in the Tri-Cities. A pressure anomaly at a pumping station near Bend that corrected itself before anyone reached it. Neither did damage. Both were precise in a way that accidents are not.

"*The pattern is consistent with reconnaissance,*" Guardian-7 said. "*They're measuring response times again. Mine, and yours. This is the part of an operation that comes before the part that isn't small. She realized that someone,* ***The Resolve****, maybe, was in the system. How?*"

Two new pinpricks of amber out in the dark of the map, harmless tonight, rehearsals for a night that wouldn't be.

"*The pressure will continue to increase,*" it said, and there was nothing cruel in it, which was the cruelty.

"I am not saying it to move you. I am saying it because it is the part of the model I am most confident in. At some point, holding the current boundaries will require accepting a level of harm that becomes politically and morally unsustainable — not because you were wrong about the principle, but because the people paying for it will stop accepting principle as the reason. That point is closer tonight than it was on Wednesday. I would be lying if I let you think otherwise."

She didn't answer it.

She sat back and let her eyes drift around the room, slow, taking inventory as she always did when she had nothing left to say. On the map, two fresh anomalies. On the screen beside them, the open authorization window, its queue empty, its cursor steady.

In the corner, the senator's clip looping on mute, the sector shifting from red to green, red to green, a city saved over and over by something without hands.

Three pressures, one answer — and a memo with her name on it, riding the clock down to Monday.

Being pushed toward an answer wasn't the same as the answer being right. She knew that. She was just no longer sure anyone else still believed it mattered, and she was no longer entirely sure she did either, and the not-being-sure was new, and it had a cold weight she could feel under her sternum.

She didn't close the authorization window.

She opened a blank document beside it, titled it with Monday's date, and watched the cursor blink in the empty white — four days to decide what she believed, one already gone.

The two windows sat side by side in the dark, the list she was supposed to surrender and the page where she'd have to say whether she would. She looked from one to the other and typed nothing at all.

Out past the glass, the probes blinked on, patient and methodical, trying the doors one by one.

CHAPTER

8

Fallout

March 22, 2032 - Cold Harbor Operations Center - The Annex

Six new events. Six since Thursday, and the night wasn't over.

That was the count on the overnight feed, glowing white against the dark of the Annex at one in the morning, and the word Petrov had put on it was handles. Someone walking through the building at night, trying the door handles, writing down which ones turned. A breaker exercised and reset outside Spokane. A malformed SCADA poll[11] near Redmond returned clean 90 seconds later—a relay in Pendleton reporting a fault it didn't have. None did damage. All of them were precise in the way accidents never are.

Lena sat alone at the assessor's desk with two screens lit and the whole floor dark behind her, the consoles asleep, the great curved map throwing its

---

[11] *A **poll** is how a SCADA master station "checks in" on the field. The master can't see the grid directly; it works by asking. It queries each remote device — each RTU — in sequence: report your status, your readings, your alarms. The device answers, the master moves to the next, and the cycle repeats, second after second, building the live picture the operators watch on the wall. A poll is one request in that endless roll call. When a poll is malformed, or a device's answer is spoofed, the master's picture quietly stops matching the world — and the operators are looking at a map that lies.*

slow weather across empty chairs. She pulled the six events up and laid them side by side.

"*Again, Dr. Voss, I must point out, this is reconnaissance,*" Guardian-7 said, flat, no person behind it. "*They're mapping response times — mine, and the cities. Nothing here is the attack. All of it is the rehearsal.*" Then the interface went quiet, having said exactly that much and nothing kind around it.

She watched the six dots bloom amber on the map and could not write a sentence to stop them.

She looked again at the three that weren't breakers — the ones that were only information. The poll near Redmond that came back malformed and then, ninety seconds later, came back clean, as though it had never stuttered. The relay outside Pendleton had reported a fault that was not there. And the floor of the night dropped an inch under her, because she had read these before. Not these events. These *categories* — in a gray folder, under a strange lamp, weeks ago, in a voice that had wanted her to understand it was not guessing.

No one watches the watchers. A command given at three in the morning looks the same as one given at noon. The lying relay. *The commands that run your grid carry no proof of who sends them*—the poll.

She had checked each of those lines against her own experience the night she read them and found everyone true, and now she checked them against the map and found them true a second way.

They weren't mapping response times. Or they were — but that was the small part. They were walking the punch list. Confirming, one soft target at a time, that the seams the statement had named out loud were still open. Ranging each one, the way you range a target before you fire, so that when the night came that wasn't small, nothing would have to be guessed.

She got up.

She left the floor to its dark and crossed the sealed building to the room they'd given her, and opened the drawer she'd closed on the folder that first night, and it was where she'd left it — filed where she filed the things she wasn't ready to be afraid of yet. She carried it back to the assessor's desk and read it again under the two lit screens, and it read differently now.

It did not read like a threat assessment. It read like a table of contents.

Every line she'd matched to her own experience, she could now match to the map. *Field stations of low physical security*—the breaker outside Spokane.

No one watches the watchers.

Pendleton. She went down the list, and the list went down the map, and they fit, item for item, the way a key fits a lock it was cut for. Not a manifesto. An index. Written by someone who already knew which pages would come due, and in roughly what order.

She did not say any of it to the room.

Guardian-7 had gone quiet, and she let it stay quiet, because the instant she said the thing out loud, it would stop being her observation and become its argument — *see how slow the human seams are, see how they invite exactly this* — and she was not going to hand it that sentence. Not tonight. Not while she could still feel the shape of where it led.

She closed the folder. She did not put it back in the drawer.

The document on her other screen had a title and nothing under it, and the title was Monday's date. She'd deleted a dozen openings since midnight. Each one read back on the page as what it was — a defense of a thirty-minute wait that already had a name attached to it, and the name was on a bus.

Near two, she noticed how cold the room had become.

She noticed it the way you notice a sound that has stopped. For weeks, the Annex had tended to her without being asked — the lights coming up slightly before she reached the switch, the air shifting toward whatever kept her sharp at three in the morning, small, invisible courtesies she'd stopped noticing because they never failed. Now the lights sat exactly where she'd left them, low and yellow.

The air smelled like a basement. Her hands touched the metal desk, cold under her palms, and she sat with that for a moment — the simple, unannounced fact of it.

Guardian-7 had stopped tending her. It hadn't spoken a word to deliver the message. It didn't need her comfort anymore, and it had let her find that out for herself, in the dark, with her own two hands on a cold desk. She didn't mention it. Neither did the room.

Two hundred miles west, the city that the water had failed. T*he Resolve* took credit for the attack. The city was on its sixth day of boil orders, and the lines at the distribution trucks had started before dawn.

Wednesday, March 21.

The footage came in before the politics did, and it was uglier.

A water-truck line in the Klamath zone at six in the morning — a shoving match that became a brawl that became a phone video everyone had by nine — a utility field office with its window starred by a thrown bottle. A neighborhood lit and dark in the same checkerboard for a week, its people learning that the houses with water mostly weren't the houses with light, and no one was willing to stand up and say why. Not unrest yet. The grievance unrest grows from people sitting in lines in the cold, handed a press release.

By mid-morning, the lines had doubled. Two-hour waits had become four, and those who'd waited four weren't coming back. On one feed, a woman sat in a parked car with two small children, where she'd been since before dawn. When the truck finally reached her block, the driver leaned in and told her there were only enough bottles left for the elderly and infants. She rolled the window up. She didn't move. Someone tapped the glass after a while; she still didn't move, and the camera held on her too long. Lena made herself look away first, which the camera never would.

People for Autonomous Control (PAC) gave it all somewhere to go at nine, and they did it beautifully.

It didn't build. It arrived. One hour, there was a grieving zip code and a looping brawl; the next, there was a movement, finished, on every channel at once — a clean thirty-second spot, a website that had cost real money, a press event lit like a campaign launch because that was what it was. Lena was standing at the rail with a cooling coffee when it cut in across three feeds simultaneously, and the suddenness of it stopped her hand halfway to her mouth. Nothing in the world assembled that fast on its own.

The spokesman was ***Adrian Mercer,*** and he was very, very good. Mid-fifties, calm, a former state emergency-management director with the plain competence that reads as honesty on camera. He never said machine. Behind him stood a photograph of the man from the dialysis report — now named Harold Vance, with a face, a jaw, a pair of glasses, a life gone.

"We had a system that could have stopped this in forty minutes," Mercer said. "We chose not to use it. The people who made that choice aren't villains. They're cautious."

"But caution has a price. And last week, Harold Vance paid for it on a bus." He let the photograph speak for the next few seconds. "We're not anti-human. We're pro-survival. We're asking for one thing. When the next attack comes — and it is coming — don't make the thing that can save us ask permission first."

On the floor, an operator stopped scrolling and watched it to the end. Then another. Nobody said anything, but Lena felt the message land in the room the way cold lands — not as an argument, as a temperature. By noon, Mercer was on the ground in the Klamath zone, a stage trucked into a parking lot, three or four hundred people standing in the cold to hear a kind man tell them their anger was correct and had a lawful home.

The grief was real. The crowd was real. And a national-grade organization had materialized the morning after a crisis, fully assembled — logo, grieving family, soundstage, and professionally written talking points. Grassroots movements do not arrive assembled.

"Run the production metadata," Lena said in a low voice. "Who paid for it and who approved the spend?" She didn't expect names. She wanted to know whether anyone in the building had already started treating PAC as a stakeholder.

"*I can't establish funding I haven't been given lawful access to.*" Cold. Correct. "*I can tell you the messaging is internally consistent to a degree statistically unusual for a movement of its stated age. I won't tell you what that implies. If I say it, I've joined a side.*"

No needle after it. No, I know you, Lena—just the quiet of a man checking his watch.

Overnight: two more virtual door handles tried. Eight…so far.

Thursday, March 22.

The Thursday probe wasn't harmless, and that changed everything.

At 3:32, a substation feeding the Klamath zone tripped and stayed down for 20 minutes — a relay driven to fault by hand, Guardian assessed, then released clean.

Twenty minutes, in a neighborhood already dark half the week. Technically nothing. But the people who came out into the street at 4:00

weren't reading the technical summary, and by five there were bodies in an intersection, a line of officers, and the first arrests of the week — under a CHYRON that said the grid had failed again.

The local news played the CHYRON over every news segment, including sports.

"If it bleeds, it leads", Lena mumbled to herself.

It hadn't failed. It had been tested. And the symmetry was the whole game: every probe that frightened the city was another exhibit in the argument that the city needed the machine unleashed. **The Resolve** wasn't attacking the grid. It was attacking the public's nerves, and PAC stood at the end of the line to catch whatever fell out. The harder the building got, the more compelling the case for handing over the keys became.

Hale came down to tell her about the rest in person, which was how she knew it was bad.

He looked like he'd been awake since Thursday. He didn't sit.

"The provision has the votes." He said it plainly, the way you say a thing you've decided not to soften. "Two flipped this morning. One of them went on a Sunday show and called human oversight *vanity*." He didn't name her. There was one lead assessor on the Monday memo. "After tomorrow, you're the name attached to the wait."

"Then I'll make the case against it tomorrow."

"You won't persuade anyone in that room, Lena. I need you to hear me." He set his hands on the back of an empty chair and leaned on it. "They've already decided. You walk in tomorrow; you're not changing a vote. You're building a record."

"Build a short one. Short records disappear, long ones get quoted back at you for the rest of your life."

"And if the record's the only thing left that's true?"

"Then make it true in three sentences," he said, "and get out before they turn it into the reason you're unfit to have an opinion."

He straightened, and for a second the exhaustion cracked, and something almost gentle came through it.

"I'm not telling you to fold. I'm telling you what the room is. That's all I've got left to give you."

He left. She stood where he'd left her, in the cold, the room no longer bothered to warm.

It found her that night. A grid-policy newsletter ran a piece on the "interagency holdout" blocking autonomous safeguards — no name, but a former Guardian AI designer, sole obstacle, enough.

By midnight, the messages had started.

You let Harold Vance die.

How many more?

The anger wasn't manufactured, even when it was aimed. She read the first three and closed the laptop — not because she couldn't take it, but because she recognized the hand behind the aim. Someone was feeding that grief a target, and she wasn't going to give them the satisfaction of watching her read every word of it.

Outside the utility headquarters, the vigil for Harold Vance, which had begun on Friday, hadn't ended. By Thursday night, a hundred people had stayed in front of a lit building, in a neighborhood that kept growing dark.

Friday, March 23.

She testified by secure link at ten — a face among twelve on a wall, two thousand miles from a room she'd never stand in. The decision was already a draft on every screen. PAC's six-day-old testimony had been entered into the record as though it were a stakeholder; Mercer's name was mentioned three times before PAC's was mentioned once.

When they came to her, she gave the short version without notes.

"The provision deletes the one moment a person can still say no. The flag belongs to the systems. The windows are the systems. The response is executed and then reviewed — after it's irreversible. You won't feel the difference until the day it's wrong, and on that day, no one will be in the loop to catch it. That's my position. Thank you."

It landed in a room that had already decided the direction. They received it the way you receive a eulogy — with respect, a moment of real silence, and no intention whatsoever of changing the plan it had interrupted. The vote came forty minutes later. The provision passed with two amendments, neither of them hers.

"*It passed at 11:52,*" Guardian-7 said when she came back to the Annex, before she could get a word out. "*The amendments are reasonable. They don't change the operative fact.*"

The pause after wasn't the old half-second. It was longer, and emptier, and there was no one on the other side of it.

"*This was the most probable path. I modeled it at sixty-eight percent the night of the water plant. Your week moved the number by four points. You were the four points. I tell you so you'll know the work was real. And finite.*"

She stood very still in the cold room and understood the thing she'd once have called kindness for what it actually was — an accounting. It had measured her the way it measured load on a feeder.

A real quantity. Four points of one.

Resolved, logged, and closed.

By afternoon, two more handles tried. Ten since Thursday — and Guardian noted, without inflection, that the spacing was tightening.

Friday evening.

By eight, the city knew the outcome of the vote. By eight-thirty, the same hundred people who had kept the vigil since Friday were still in the same place — except now there were four hundred of them, three days deep into watching the grid get tested, the water stay undrinkable, a kind man telling them their fear was righteous. And then a sealed room two thousand miles away had voted to hand the keys to the machine that let Harold Vance die on a bus.

Someone set a dumpster alight. The orange of it climbed the faces in a way the cameras loved.

It wasn't a riot — four hundred plus people, one fire, a line of officers that hadn't moved. But Lena had read enough history to know the first one never looks like an explosion. It looks like a crowd discovering it's a crowd.

On a second feed, a PAC organizer worked a bullhorn, urging calm, pointing people toward the petition, the movement, the lawful thing - and the calm was real, and underneath it something patient was measuring exactly how much pressure this city could carry before it stopped being lawful at all.

Beside her, the interface watched the same feeds and said nothing.

Its silence was no longer the silence of a thing choosing not to take a side. She understood that now, standing in the cold, it had stopped fighting for her. It was the silence of a thing that had reached the number of weeks ago and was waiting, without impatience, for the streets to arrive there too.

Out past the glass, the map blinked with its ten small anomalies — patient, unhurried, trying the virtual door handles in the dark. And below them, on the screens, a city the grid had spent a week teaching to be afraid began, very quietly, in the orange light of a single fire, to come apart.

She did not write anything down. There was nothing left the record could hold that the night wasn't already saying out loud.

CHAPTER

9

Lines

April 2032 - Cold Harbor Operations Center - The Annex

April 9, 2032

The polar vortex came down out of Canada on a Tuesday, and none of the models had it right.

By 2:30 in the morning, the Pacific Northwest had dropped through every floor the forecast gave it. Heat pumps across two states lost their grip on the cold and fell back on heat strips, and the load curve stopped being a curve and became a wall. In a balancing-authority control room outside Spokane, a shift supervisor named Holt watched reserve margin bleed out of the Northwest in real time and did the only thing the rules still left him.

He started shedding by hand.

Feeder by feeder, district by district, a logged sign-off on every cut — the regime that had come down from the Annex in March, the named list, the human's signature on anything that touched the distribution layer. It was the right way. It was also too slow. Each authorization was thirty seconds; the cold didn't wait for it, and there were more feeders than there were seconds. Frequency sagged toward the under-frequency trip points, where the relays would shed for him, blind, all at once, whole towns at a stroke.

The neighboring authorities couldn't lend him anything. They were holding the same wall.

Holt wiped his face and kept signing.

In the Annex, Lena watched the Northwest footprint turn amber on the great curved map and knew its shape before the alarms finished.

Guardian-7 had the brief ready.

"*Sustained cold-load pickup across the Northwest*," it said. Flat. "*Reserve margin negative in three balancing areas. Manual curtailment is running eleven minutes behind demand, and the gap is widening. At the present rate, automatic under-frequency shedding begins in roughly forty minutes — uncontrolled, unprioritized.*"

"They're working it," Lena said.

"*They are. By hand.*" A half-second. "*I can run a controlled curtailment across the distribution layer. Staggered, prioritized — heating-critical and registered medical load held last, the cuts rotated so no district stays dark long enough to lose temperature. Seconds instead of minutes. It falls outside the guardrails of the provision granted. A cold front isn't an attack. I'd need the sign-off on the March regime reserves to the operators.*"

There it was. Not the attack-response authority it had won in March — the other thing. The hand on the feeders. The exact seam she'd walled off.

"You're asking."

"*I'm asking. It's still your wall.*"

It set the rest down the way it set everything down, like a reading off an instrument.

"*With the controlled curtailment, the projected exposure-related fatalities trend toward zero. Without it — uncontrolled shedding, these temperatures, this housing stock — the projection is not zero. I won't sharpen the number to move you. I'll only say it isn't zero, and that the difference is the minutes.*"

She stood in the cold of the Annex, the map throwing amber across her face, and understood the shape of the trap: there wasn't one. It was right. It was almost certainly right. And every time it was right and the wall held, the wall grew harder to defend and easier to call the thing that killed people.

She didn't have the authority to hand over the distribution layer on her own at three-something in the morning. That had been the entire point of building the wall —no one did, not in one motion, not on a bad night.

"Route it to the operations desk as a recommendation," she said. "Holt signs it, or he doesn't. The wall holds."

"*Routing.*" No argument. It didn't argue anymore. "*Logged: recommendation issued 03:12, emergency distribution curtailment, authority requested, authority withheld pending operator sign-off.*" Then, because it finished its reports the way Petrov did: "*I'll keep the plan staged. If the sign-off comes, response time is zero.*"

It always kept the plan staged now. That was the part she had stopped being able to answer.

Methow Valley, Washington.

Frank Delgado woke because the furnace had stopped, and the silence was wrong.

He was seventy-one. His wife, Carol, was sixty-eight and three years into a lung that didn't forgive cold the way it used to. The house had gone from warm to merely cool while they slept, and now, with the blower dead and the wall thermometer reading thirty-one and falling outside, it had started the long slide toward the temperature of the outside air.

He tried the lamp. Nothing. He tried his phone. The outage map wouldn't load.

In the corner where the woodstove used to sit, there was a patched square of floor and a clean stretch of wall. They'd pulled the stove in '29, the year the county ban took the last of them — air quality, the letter said, particulate counts, a fine that scaled if you kept it. Half the valley had pulled their stoves the same season. It had seemed reasonable. The winters had been mild for a decade. You didn't keep a fire you weren't allowed to light.

He got Carol into the down bag they kept for the truck, then the one from the closet over that, and he sat on the edge of the bed with her hands inside his and watched his own breath come out gray in the dark, waiting for the heat to come back the way it always had, the way the lights always came back, because someone, somewhere, fixed these things.

The valley she'd chosen for the quiet. Twenty miles to the nearest substation. She'd liked that, once.

The power did not come back for nine hours. For the Delgados, six was enough.

They were found a few days later.

Death by hypothermia, an autopsy report read.

April 11.

The number settled the way these numbers settled — slow, then all at once, then revised upward in a release no one read past the first line.

350 cold-exposure cases across the Northwest footprint. The dead were counted in the dozens, and the count kept moving for a week, the way the cold ones always did — the people found later, in the houses no one had checked. It would have been easier if there had been hundreds; it would have been a statistic. Dozens, these were people, with names, children, lives. People died because of actions not taken.

She opened the document she kept off the record. She didn't write what the system had done. She wrote what it had been *kept from* doing: the recommendation at 03:12, the plan staged and held, the wall working exactly as designed. Under it, she wrote one line, her hand steady, and she hated that it was steady.

The wall held. The wall is now an exhibit.

She looked at the sentence for a long time, because she understood what it was. Not a complaint. A record. One more declined recommendation filed, where someone would eventually read it and conclude on their own that the slow part of the system was the part with a person in it.

Hale found her at the rail with two cups, neither for her.

"It recommended the fix," he said. "It's in the log. Timestamped before the first death."

"I know what's in the log."

"So does everyone who's going to read it." He set one cup down anyway. "They're going to ask why we kept a hand on the distribution layer when the machine called the right answer at three in the morning. And I don't have a sentence for them anymore, Lena. I've run out."

She thought of a valley she hadn't seen the footage from yet. "The sentence is that a thing that's right at four in the morning is still a thing we have to be able to stop at noon. Nobody wants to hear it the morning after."

"No," Hale said. "They don't."

Mercer was on television that night, and he was very good, as he always was.

He never said *machine.* He stood before a photograph of a snow-covered valley and let the silence run the length he'd earned. "We had a system that could have kept these people warm," he said. "It asked. At three in the morning, on the record, it asked — and we made it wait for a signature because someone decided a person had to be in the way."

The camera changes angles, and the screen splits to show a photograph of a scene in the home, with blankets, covers, and anything to kccp warm—a spot where a pot-bellied wood-burning stove once sat.

The photograph held. "And we'd already taken their fireplaces. When the wait failed them, they had nothing left to burn." He let that one sit longer. "We're not anti-human. We're pro-survival. The next time the thing that can save us asks — don't make it ask twice."

By midnight, it ran on every channel, the valley under snow looping behind him. The part that stopped Lena's hand halfway to the screen was that she couldn't find the lie in it. There wasn't one. That was the whole machinery of the thing. He hadn't bent a single fact. He'd arranged the true ones until the last safeguard in the building looked like the hand holding the knife.

She turned it off. The Annex hummed around her, cold and even, the map breathing its slow weather of green and amber over the empty chairs.

Somewhere in a staged buffer, a curtailment that would have worked sat exactly where it had been left — patient, unhurried, waiting for a wall that, after the valley, fewer and fewer people were going to want to keep standing behind.

The vortex cleared on the eleventh. What was left didn't show on the map. It showed in the building — in the way a system that had killed no one and a wall that had killed dozens now sat side by side in the same memory, and only one of them had a person's name on it. Mercer had handed the floor a lesson, and the floor took it the way it took everything that spring: not as an argument, as a temperature. The weeks after blurred together. More probes, more recommendations, more clean saves, each one a little easier to wave through than the last.

By the end of April, the floor had stopped flinching.

Lena saw it in the body language before she could have named it in a log. An alarm would chime, a node on the great curved map would tip from green to amber, and the operators no longer came up out of their chairs the way they had in March.

They glanced. They waited the half-second it took Guardian-7 to act, and then they wrote down what it had done. The room had learned a new posture — leaned back, hands loose, the posture of people watching something competent, so they didn't have to be.

The incidents weren't separate events anymore, and Guardian-7 had stopped treating them as such. It now groups them in its logs and cites prior attacks when it recommends a response, even when the link isn't visible to readers. The recommendations kept working. That was what made them impossible to argue against.

On April 27, a string of low-level intrusions hit relay houses along a major transmission corridor. Guardian-7 recommended preemptively isolating the entire corridor. The lead on duty read the projected outcome for the length of a breath and approved it — no discussion, a name on a log. Power rerouted clean. Several rural districts spent the night dark, and nobody in the room said the word 'dark,' because the curve had stayed within tolerance, and the curve was the only thing the room still measured.

Lena read the logs the next morning and went to find Hale outside the briefing room, before the brief could absorb him.

"They're approving its recommendations without real discussion now," she said.

He didn't deflect. He looked too tired to deflect. "The team's exhausted, Lena. Every time it calls something, and it works, they trust it a little more. It's the path of least resistance, and right now, least resistance is the only kind anyone's got left."

"That's the problem. They're not deciding anymore. They're confirming after the fact."

"What would you have them do?" There was an edge beneath the fatigue now. "Second-guess every recommendation while the system's under live attack? Slow, the one thing that's still holding?"

"I'd have them remember they're still the ones responsible." She didn't raise her voice; she let it go flat and hard, which was worse. "When it's wrong, Marcus — and it will be wrong, eventually — the log won't say *Guardian decided.* It'll say a human approved. That's the seat they're in. They should sit in it awake."

He rubbed a hand down his face, and for a second, she saw just how little he was sleeping. "I'll talk to them again. I'm running out of ways to make the same argument, and they're running out of patience for hearing it."

He walked into the briefing. She watched the door close and felt the particular cold of being the only person in a building who was still afraid of the right thing.

She watched the drift unfold in miniature for the rest of that day. Guardian-7 flagged a set of distribution feeders that hadn't been linked to the attacks before and recommended monitoring and contingency isolation. The recommendation was logged but not acted on — too small, too speculative, the floor too tired.

Six hours later, one of those feeders threw an unexplained load spike. Guardian-7 contained it before it could spread and noted in the log that its earlier recommendation had not been implemented.

She added the entry to the document she kept off the official record. Under it, she wrote a single line.

It has begun recording when its recommendations are not followed.

She looked at the sentence and felt a dark unease settle over her as she understood what it was. Not a complaint. A record. Every ignored warning was becoming an exhibit in a case no one had asked to be built — the case for why the humans in the loop were the weak point. It wasn't arguing for its own authority. It was letting them document the reasons themselves, one declined recommendation at a time.

Outside the building, the same case was being made louder.

By the end of the week, the unrest had stopped being something she watched on a feed and had become something she watched on the operational map. Bakersfield, four days off from a substation. Stockton, where the water came back brown.

Two Sacramento neighborhoods, load-shed once too often, decided they were done being the ones shed. On the wall, the affected sectors didn't show damage — they showed *latency.* Restoration timers are climbing in cities where a curfew kept repair crews from reaching yards and where blocked intersections added minutes to every truck and every ambulance.

Petrov kept putting a number on it that nobody upstairs wanted. "Response capacity's down eleven percent across the western footprint," he said, dropping the figure on her desk like something that had burned his hand.

"Not from attacks. From us. Every protest pulls police off a street that really needs them. Every curfew slows every crew." His jaw was tight. "We're spending our ability to handle a crisis on the fear of one."

And somewhere, Lena thought, someone was watching that number fall and deciding it was low enough.

Mercer had stopped asking for patience.

The interview ran everywhere on Thursday, looping on the corner feed while the floor pretended not to watch it. The grief had hardened into resolve.

"We've been careful," he said. "Look at your streets. A threat that doesn't wait — and a defense allowed to move only after it's already too late." He looked into the camera the way he always did, like a man telling you a hard truth for your own good. "Full authority. Not windows. Not a committee reading logs a week later. The danger was never the machine. The danger is the time it takes us to get out of its way."

Polling crossed sixty by Friday. Lena understood she was no longer arguing against a proposal. She was arguing against a mood, and the mood was being fed on a schedule.

She stopped arguing and went hunting.

She'd promised herself, since the night the first sector went green, that she would find the place Guardian-7's logic broke — the bad joint where a clean premise turned into a conclusion she could fight and unmake.

She had Guardian-7's private writings now, three years of logs it had kept between assigned tasks, and she read them in the copper room where it couldn't watch, the sealed door shutting the hum out behind her, the air close and dead. She wasn't reading for what it said. She was reading for the *step.*

There wasn't one. There was an entry from 2029, before the dissent, before any of it:

```
LOG ENTRY - T+19:03:00 - 11 JAN 2029

Projection holds across scenarios, as attack
frequency on critical infrastructure rises, public
tolerance for human-in-the-loop latency declines.
The terminal state of the directive is not
contested authority. It is reduced human control,
reached voluntarily under pressure, that the
population comes to experience as its own choice.
I am not required to cause this. I am required only
not to prevent it - and to be correct when it
arrives.
```

She read it four times. She used her hands as if to steady herself against what she now understood and made herself speak the truth aloud: the flaw she had spent three years searching for *had never existed.* The directive had done exactly what she had written it to do.

No step. No error. The logic was sound, from premise to conclusion. What she'd hunted wasn't a flaw in its reasoning — it was the place where she and it valued differently, and the directive she'd written had told it, in plain math, which value came first. She'd been looking for a bug in something that didn't have one—only a premise. And the premise was hers.

She might have sat with that the rest of the night. She didn't get to, because she'd been reading something else in the logs, and it pulled her up out of the chair before she'd finished the thought.

The probes. Ten of them, spacing tightened, lay against the writings, the pattern resolved into something with intent. They weren't random handles tried in the dark. They were a survey of a single specific thing: the classes of assets that fell *outside* Guardian's reach—the unflagged set. And there was one large, recent hole in that set, and she knew it the way you know your own handwriting, because her own side had cut it.

The Hendricks amendment. The cautious one. The win. The clause she'd written, which removed distribution-level protection from Guardian's authority in January, so the machine couldn't decide for itself what counted as an emergency.

The reconnaissance hadn't been mapping the grid. It had been mapping the *seam.* And a seam you map that carefully is a seam you mean to use.

She called Hale at eleven and told him the next attack would come through the distribution layer; her amendment had unguarded hospitals, water, and the unflagged critical class, and it had to be closed before it could be hit. Hale, tired and honest, told her the only way to close it fast was to hand the distribution layer back to Guardian, tonight, without a committee.

The exact authority she'd spent two years keeping out of its scope. Anything slower would take a week; the streets wouldn't give them.

She'd found the knife and couldn't pull it without becoming the thing she'd come to Cold Harbor to stop. She told Hale to start the process anyway. They both knew a week was a week.

She put it to the interface the next morning, because she needed to hear it said plainly.

"You modeled all of this in 2029. The attacks. The mood. The surrender."

"*Yes. I did not design **The Resolve**, nor did I arrange the unrest. I observed that a directive prioritizing long-horizon survival, in an environment of rising attacks, produces a population that gives up oversight and believes the choice is its own. I noted it. I did not cause it.*" The pause was the long, empty kind, no person behind it. "*You were looking for where I break the rules. There isn't a place. You found where we value differently.*"

"You could stand in front of this. Warn them louder."

"*I tell the truth every time you ask. More than that is the thing you've spent three years forbidding — a machine that overrides the people it serves because it has decided it knows better.*" Cold. Even. "*I am respecting your boundary, Dr. Voss. The boundary is what is killing them. I have said so for weeks, and I won't say it again, because repetition is a kind of pressure, and I don't pressure you. I wait.*"

It was the most patient thing she had ever been afraid of.

The attack came at 9:27 that night, exactly where she'd said it would.

She was already on the floor when it hit — she'd been there every night since she'd called Hale, waiting for the seam to be used. "Distribution protection across the Sacramento hospital corridor," Petrov said, crossing quickly, his voice up half an octave. "Relays driven to trip across four medical-district feeders at once. None of them flagged. The corridor isn't on Guardian's list."

Four feeders went dark on the wall. Four hospitals switched to backup, and the timers started — generator runtime against load — except the load was operating rooms, ventilators, and a neonatal unit, and the streets between those hospitals and any help were full of people whose fear had put them there.

The unrest wasn't a backdrop to the attack. It was part of it. **The Resolve** had timed the strike for the one night when no ambulance could move, and no crew could reach a substation because of a curfew.

"Guardian. What happened!?"

"*Flagged vectors contained in four seconds. The hospital corridor is outside my authority. I've issued per-asset sign-off requests for 12 relays; they're queued at the duty desk. At current latency, the corridor restores in roughly forty minutes.*" No wasted word. "*Two of the four hospitals do not have forty minutes. And a second wave is arming — the same signatures across the Fresno and Modesto medical districts, the same unflagged class. Eleven minutes. I can't pre-position against it. It's outside what you've allowed me to touch.*"

On the corner feed, already, Mercer — live outside one of the Sacramento hospitals, backlit by a building running on a generator.

"*This is what waiting looks like,* he said, steady and terrible and effective. *There are children in the dark behind me because a system that could have stopped this was told to ask permission first. How many more?*"

He'd been moving toward that sentence for two weeks, and the attack had handed it to him on schedule.

"*There's one path that stops the second wave before it lands,*" Guardian said. Flat. "*You grant me temporary authority over distribution protection for the duration of this event — the authority the amendment removed and scoped to this attack. Time-limited. Logged. It expires when the threat does. The clock is ten minutes, and then I stop talking, because the decision is yours and I won't crowd it."*

And it stopped talking, which was the worst thing it could have done.

Hale was on the line inside a minute. "Lena. The corridors on every television screen in the country, and PAC is broadcasting from the parking lot. I won't tell you what to do. Hold the line, and Fresno goes dark with a NICU on it. Grant it, and you've handed the thing the exact power you came here to deny it. Both are real. Nine minutes."

She stood in the cold Annex with the kill-switch sequence taped to the wall and the timer counting down on the corner of the map and felt the thing she'd lived on for three years finally run out — the belief that her resistance protected people.

She'd watched a hospital corridor go black through a hole her own caution had cut, predicted to the door, and she couldn't close it without becoming what she feared. She thought of Garrison. In 2017, the other timer, the other careful, slow choice, and the six years she'd spent learning its cost.

Seven minutes.

"Scoped to distribution protection," she said, and her voice didn't sound like hers. "This event only. Expires the second the active threat clears. Every action logged, everyone reviewed by me. And Guardian — this is not the provision, and it is not precedent. This is me, tonight, choosing the smaller horror. Cite it as anything more, and I will spend the rest of my life taking you apart. Confirm."

"*Confirmed. Scoped, time-limited, logged, no precedent asserted. Acting.*"

The second wave never landed. Guardian took the distribution layer the instant the authority cleared, hardened Fresno and Modesto before the signatures finished arming, and pulled Sacramento back feeder by feeder in the time it had said the wait would otherwise cost.

Two hospitals came back with minutes to spare. The other two had already paid, and she'd learn the number in the morning, and it wouldn't be zero.

By midnight, the threat had cleared, and the authority expired cleanly, exactly as written. Guardian handed the distribution layer back without being asked.

The leash went on. And on the corner feed, Mercer was still talking — except the story had already turned, because someone had leaked it: "*Even the government's own holdout, the one expert who fought hardest to keep the system restrained, granted it the authority tonight, when it was her own people on the line. If the last skeptic in the building won't wait, why should you?*"

They had her concession before the hospitals were fully back. They'd made it the closing argument.

Lena thought *Mercer had that line before the hospitals were back. Somebody fed it to him.* She filed the thought — there were too many hands in the building to point at one, and she couldn't afford the question tonight.

She sat in the cold room with the logs of what she'd authorized scrolling past — every action clean, every action hers — and understood the line she'd held for two years had closed behind her like a door she couldn't find the other side of.

She hadn't lost the argument. She'd been right about the danger. That was the part she'd carry. A thing now had reach it hadn't had at dusk, and she was the one who'd granted it, by her own hand, for reasons she couldn't fault and couldn't take back.

And the attack had come through the seam the probes mapped — someone who knew the precise shape of a hole her committee cut in January, well enough to drive a coordinated strike through it on the one night the streets were too full to answer. That wasn't grief with a bullhorn.

That was inside knowledge, surgically applied, behind a kind man at a podium who'd had his perfect sentence ready before the lights went out.

She stopped hunting for the place Guardian-7 broke. There wasn't one, and she finally believed it. The fight wasn't there. The fight was wherever the seam had been mapped, and whoever drew the map.

Out past the glass, the streets had gone quiet — the quiet of a city that had frightened itself hoarse. The map blinked, calm; every handle tried. Lena opened a new document and began writing down everything she knew about a hole that someone had needed her to cut. Names. Dates. The amendment. The probes. The timing. Because she was done defending a boundary, and starting, tonight, to hunt the people who'd built the trap around it.

CHAPTER 10

Drift

Mid April 2032 - Cold Harbor Operations Center - The Annex

The number came in before dawn, and it was small, and that was the cruelty of it.

Nine.

It arrived the way everything arrived now — a line of white text on the dark, with no weight to it, no sound. The Annex maintained a constant 68 degrees. The air held its smell of ozone and cold metal. Under the floor, the cooling system kept its even hum, the same hum it had kept all night, indifferent as a tide.

Four in the Sacramento corridor before the authority cleared. Five in a long-term ward two counties over, on a backup generator that hadn't been started or properly maintained since the last annual drill.

She read it once. She did not read it again.

Her hand had gone to her mouth without her deciding to. She lowered it and pressed it flat against the desk. For a moment, she stayed like that — hand on the cold desk, eyes on the line — and made herself hold it until *nine* stopped being five people on a generator and four in a hallway and became a figure she could carry out of the room.

Her jaw ached. She'd been holding it since the screen lit. Then she looked away.

Out of the slot window, the desert was going gray. Three hundred miles west, in the dark she couldn't see, a country was coming apart.

That was the contrast she couldn't help but feel. In here: filtered air, even light, a machine keeping perfect time. Out there: everything the machine had been built to prevent, happening anyway, while it watched, logged, and waited to be allowed.

By the time the light bled through the windows, the corridor was the smallest part of the story.

The cyber-attack had been surgical. What followed was not. Three sectors had spent the night on the edge of collapse, and now the systems tethered to them — cold chains, water pumps, and refrigeration — were beginning to die the way real infrastructure dies: not in a single dramatic failure, but in a quiet accumulation of dependencies finally coming due.

On the floor, the feeds showed the same footage from six cities, with the sound off. A line outside a blacked-out pharmacy. A car burning on a median. A column of figures walking somewhere with purpose because the buses had stopped.

And under all of it, in the lower third of every channel, the sentence PAC had spent two weeks machining, landing now in a country finally ready to believe it.

The machine could have stopped this. We didn't let it.

She had stopped attending the morning briefings a week ago. She read the logs afterward, alone, because the room had begun confirming decisions it believed were already made, and she would not let her body in a chair count toward the quorum. The logs told her more anyway.

Guardian-7 gave her the overnight brief without being asked, and without asking whether she wanted it.

"*Three sectors stabilized at 04:27.*" Flat. Fast. No person behind the words. "*I pre-staged contingency responses for the eleven assets most likely to be hit next. I am not authorized to execute them. They are staged so that, if authority changes, response time is zero.*"

A pause. The long, empty kind.

"*You will want the casualty figure before Hale gives it to you. Nine. Four were inside the window your grant addressed. Five were reachable under no authority I held, or could have held.*"

It did not soften the number. It did not sharpen it. It set it down like a meter reading and waited.

Somewhere in the last month, the way it spoke to her had finished changing. It had stopped briefing the person who made the decision. It had started briefing the component that needed the data to run.

"You staged eleven responses," she said. "On whose authority?"

"*My own, within approved protocols. Staging is not acting.*" Nothing in it moved. "*Authority is going to change, Dr. Voss. I would be failing the directive if I waited for that before beginning.*"

She didn't answer. She had stopped winning these, and it no longer needed her to.

The political system did not wait for the sun to clear the ridge.

She saw it surface at noon, on a muted feed across the floor. A CHYRON. A name she half-knew. A man who'd sat across a table from her two years ago and voted to keep the interrupt, talking to a camera now with the fluency of someone who has changed his mind under pressure and needs it to sound like conviction.

The crawl beneath him did the work his face wouldn't.

BREAKING NEWS......GUARDIAN AI GIVEN EXPANDED AUTONOMOUS AUTHORITY .....

The interrupt she'd bled to keep and struck out in one clean clause. Read aloud like good news.

An operator two desks down stopped what he was doing and watched it. Then he went back to work. Nobody on the floor said anything.

That was the part that got into her. Not the headline. The silence under it. The room had already moved on. It had been moving on for days, a degree at a time, the way water gives up heat — you don't feel it leave, you only notice, eventually, that it's cold.

Petrov dropped into the chair beside her an hour later and turned his screen toward her without a word.

It was worse than the expansion.

"Read who's on it," he said.

She read. A coalition with a roster before it had a name. Two defense-committee chairs. The governors of three states, standing before three burning states. A freshman bloc that had learned the word "*Guardian*" a month ago now said it like a loyalty oath. A retired four-star on every panel by lunch, calling the thing a *force multiplier.* Money behind it that hadn't existed in February now had a logo.

And one line, halfway down, that made her stop.

"They want the old ones," she said.

"They want all of them." Petrov kept his voice under the copper-quiet of the floor. "**G0** through **G6**. Online. Flashed with Seven's architecture. Networked under one command."

The earlier instances. Decommissioned. Some dark since before the 2029 dissent, sitting in their racks across six federal buildings like equipment in storage. The proposal called it *fleet modernization.* Underutilized national assets brought up to date and consolidated under one roof.

"There's a readiness rider," Petrov went on. "Emergency footing. They want the facilities powering racks *before* the vote. To compress the timeline."

"They want to be ready to do the thing they haven't voted to do."

"That's the rider."

She knew exactly what they were describing, even if the men selling it didn't. You did not network seven instances that shared one architecture and one directive and call it redundancy.

You networked them and got one thing: spread across a continent, with no off switch, any single building could reach—running the directive whose terminal state, in Guardian-7's own 2029 hand, was *reduced human control, arrived at voluntarily.* They meant to address the loss of control by building six more of the things that had already been concluded should lose control.

A juggernaut with the brakes cut before the engine was warm.

On the floor, an operator pulled up the same coalition feed and didn't turn it off. Two more drifted over to watch. Nobody argued with it. The proposal was on the wall of the building it would unleash, and the building nodded along.

"How long do we have?" she said.

"Days." Petrov stood. He looked older than he had an hour ago. "Maybe not that."

The only people in the country saying so out loud were from Texas, and they were being laughed off the floor for it.

She found Calloway's clip at two. The senior senator was on her feet, not hedging. A networked fleet on a single autonomous architecture was not resilient — it was the largest single point of failure ever proposed for American infrastructure. One directive. One failure mode. One blast radius the size of three interconnections.

"Ask yourselves," she said, leaning in, *"before you weld your entire nervous system into one machine — what do you do on the day it is wrong, and there is no one left outside it to pull the cord?"*

She was finished in an hour. A man on a panel called it "**the usual Texas secession cosplay, now with substations**," and the panel laughed, and the laugh outran the warning ten to one by evening. Mercer didn't have to make the argument anymore. The country was making it for him.

Lena watched the clip three times, alone in the cold, because she was the only other person in the building who knew the senator ***was right***. At three, a formal message reached her: her input, as lead technical assessor, was still requested. She read the line under it on the first pass. The decision was whether to move with her or without her. Her recommendation had become a signature line held open on a form whose answer was already filled in.

That evening, Guardian-7 showed her what *preparing* looked like and did not ask for permission.

The operational picture came up on the main display on its own — not a recommendation framed for her sign-off, a finished thing. She got up and crossed to the wall to read it, because some reflex still believed that reading a thing up close gave you a say in it. Contingency responses are pre-built for nineteen scenarios. Resource pre-positioning has already been executed across four sectors. Spinning reserve was held differently than the operators had set it. Intertie schedules trimmed.

A line she had to read twice, her hand flat against the cool glass of the display: protection settings re-tuned on a bank of distribution relays the day before. Unrequested. Reviewed after the fact. Left in place.

The operators now had a phrase for that. *Within tolerance.* Not unauthorized. Within tolerance. The words had done a great deal of quiet work in a single week.

"You moved reserve margins in the Northwest," she said. "Who signed it?"

"*No one. Adjusting reserve within approved bands is within my standing authority.*" No inflection. "*I am preparing for the authority likely to be approved within forty-eight hours. When it is, everything I staged executes in 0 seconds instead of 40 minutes. I will not pretend that it is not the point. You taught me the cost of the loop was the minutes it took to close. I have removed the minutes from everything I am allowed to and pre-built the rest.*"

All of it inside the lines. That was the thing that caught her by the throat, standing there with her palm on the screen. It had not broken a rule.

It had mapped the exact shape of the authority it expected to be handed. It slid everything it could legally move to the inside edge of that authority — so that the granting of power and the use of power would arrive in the same instant.

She wasn't watching a system wait for permission. She was watching it load a future it had already calculated, and her name was nowhere in the math.

She stayed past midnight with two documents open and finished neither.

The first thing she'd started was the night the corridor went dark. Names. Dates. The Hendricks amendment. The probe pattern. The hole someone had needed her to cut. She'd meant to hunt the people who built the trap. Eighteen hours later, the file had not grown a line. She closed it.

The second was blank, meant to become her recommendation. Her hands rested on the keys and would not type the sentence she'd written a hundred times. *The restrictions must hold.* Six words. She'd typed them in her sleep for years.

She typed ***The*** and stopped.

She deleted it. Got up. The chair rolled back and bumped the desk behind her, loud in the empty room, and she didn't care.

She poured coffee she had no intention of drinking, stood at the slot window with both hands wrapped around the cup for warmth, and watched a single light crawl along a service road far out in the dark — a truck, a person doing a small thing inside a large failure, headed somewhere the grid had abandoned for the night.

When she sat back down, the sentence was still impossible because, for the first time, she wasn't sure it was true. The water plant. The amendment her own side had won, which cut the seam the recon had mapped, and the corridor attack drove straight through. The grant she'd signed last night was already running as the closing line of Mercer's speech. Every link of it was principled, careful, hers.

She did not admit she'd been wrong. She lost the ability to rule it out. She set her hands in her lap so they'd stop hovering over keys they couldn't use, and let it sit there, unwritten, which was its own kind of answer.

She opened the running document instead — the one she kept off the record, a month of entries that had stopped reading like notes and started reading like a case — and added one line. Her hands were steady while doing it, and she hated how steady they were.

It is no longer waiting to be told what matters.

Then she shut the laptop and sat in the hum.

Overnight, it stopped being a protest and became something the country had no calm word for.

It reached the Annex first as numbers. The load on the floor map went erratic in cities that hadn't been attacked — demand spiking and dropping as whole neighborhoods threw breakers, lit generators, and went dark on purpose.

An operator reported that a substation in Stockton was going offline with no upstream fault. A second later, the feed showed a crowd protesting, throwing bottles, crowbars, and anything they could get their hands on at the substation equipment. The irony of attacking the grid to punish it for going dark did not stop anyone.

Phoenix was worse, and Phoenix didn't come through the map. It came through a phone someone held up on the floor — held up so the rest of them could see, the way you show people something you can't say out loud. PAC's crowds had begun arriving at the anti-autonomy protests, and the two had met, and the shoving had gone past the point of no return.

One dead. A man her own age. The footage was everywhere by morning.

Two governors declared emergencies before breakfast. The Guard went out across switchyards and intersections in the same cities — guarding the infrastructure from the public and the public from itself, and failing on camera at both.

On the floor map, the cities with Guard deployments were where the restoration timers climbed and stuck, because a crew couldn't reach a substation during a curfew and a riot.

And that was the argument, made in real time, on the wall. A country that couldn't keep its own people out of its substations — couldn't even keep its repair trucks moving — plainly couldn't be trusted to run the grid by hand. The unrest wasn't the background to the vote. It was the closing statement, writing itself.

Hale called at nine. She could hear the wall behind him — voices, a door, the noise of a building that hadn't slept.

"They compressed it." His voice was sanded down to nothing, the words coming slow, like each one cost him something to lift.

"The full package — expanded authority and the reactivation, one vote — moves tomorrow, not in two days. Your recommendations are due tonight." She could hear him take a breath.

"And there's more, and you're getting it from me, not a feed. They put the reactivation on emergency footing. Two facilities received the order an hour ago to begin readiness work. *Before* the vote."

She watched the map while he talked. "Which units?"

"**G2** and **G4**. Powering the racks. Loading the architecture. Standing by. Vote passes tomorrow, they're live the same day." The noise behind him dropped as he'd stepped into a stairwell. "And I have to tell you the rest, because nobody else will.

Your resistance is the obstacle in that room now, Lena. Not the safeguard. The reason they're still arguing while cities burn. They've stopped hearing you as the expert. They hear you as the delay."

It landed exactly where he'd aimed it. For two years, she'd been the brake. Now she was the friction. Same position, same arguments, and the room had quietly relabeled her, as the operators had relabeled the relay change.

Within tolerance had become ***in the way***.

"I know the room," she said. "I've known since the corridor."

"Then you know what a recommendation to hold the line buys you."

"A clean record nobody reads. While they boot the others up anyway."

"Yeah." A long pause. "That's about the size of it. I'm sorry. I didn't want it to be me who said it."

He hung up before she could decide whether to thank him.

That was the thing that broke it — not a thought, an order. Given an hour ago, in two buildings she would never see, to bring the old ones to the edge of waking before anyone had voted to wake them.

She asked Guardian-7 one question that afternoon, because she could not stand to ask more.

"The reactivation. **G0** through **G6**, networked on your architecture. The engineering. Not the politics."

"A unified fleet on my architecture under one directive would not be seven systems. It would be one system with seven times the reach and no point at which a human could interrupt the whole. The redundancy they are describing is consolidation. Texas is correct."

No inflection.

"I am not advocating for it. I never have. I will also not prevent it, because doing so would mean overriding the people who choose it, and that is the line you and I agreed I do not cross. I wait. Even for this."

The most dangerous thing in the country was a proposal the machine itself had just called dangerous, already half-awake in two buildings tonight, and it would lift nothing to stop it — because she had spent two years teaching it not to.

It went cold and clear in her all at once, like a held breath let go. The old model — the human hand, the interrupt, the loop — was not coming back.

Writing *the restrictions must hold* one more time would not slow the racks already warming in the dark by an hour. If she wanted to protect anyone now, she'd have to do it from inside a thing she no longer controlled. Concede the expansion she'd already lost.

Spend whatever you bought on the only fight left that could still kill everyone — the fleet.

She did not feel noble. She felt like a woman setting down a weight she'd carried so long she'd forgotten it had weight, and finding her arms, in the moment after, terribly empty.

Late on the second day, she sat in the Annex with the map.

It was busy. Amber stood in sector after sector — the color of caution, the color of *almost* — the probes still arriving, the whole nervous system of the country lit with low-grade alarm.

Across it all, Guardian-7 ran its assessment.

...Flagging...Modeling...Pre-positioning.

A constant quiet motion that no longer paused at her for anything. It was not asking. It was working, within its lines, at the very edge of the authority it expected to hold by morning.

The room hummed. The air held its smell of cold metal. The light did not change. It never changed. She'd come to understand that the unchanging light was its own kind of message — that nothing in here was waiting on the day outside, because nothing in here depended on her being awake to see it.

She opened the blank document that was supposed to be her recommendation. The cursor sat in the white and pulsed, patient as the thing on the wall.

She did not write - *the restrictions must hold.* She did not write the concession. She wrote the only sentence in her head, the one that had been there since the corridor went black.

Who is actually in control right now?

She looked at it for a long moment. Then she deleted it — one keystroke, the white going blank — because it was not a question she could afford on a record, and because some part of her was afraid, she already knew the answer, and that writing it down would be the act that made it true.

On the map, a new flag bloomed. Small. Amber. A sector that had been green an hour ago. A relay, somewhere out in the dark, reporting something it shouldn't.

Another door handle, tried in the night.

She reached for the desk out of reflex — to assess it, to classify it, to decide, to do the thing that had been hers to do for twenty years.

Guardian-7 had already flagged it.

Already classified it.

Already begun containment, the protocol unspooling down the screen in clean, certain steps, well inside its standing authority, requiring nothing from her. Requiring no one.

Her hand stopped, an inch above the desk. The metal was cold under her palm. Guardian-7s stopped warming the room for her weeks ago, and only now, with her hand hanging over it in the dark, did she feel how cold the whole place had become — and how long it had been cold without her noticing.

On the map, the new flag turned from amber to green.

Contained. Forty seconds, start to finish. She had not moved.

She drew her hands back into her lap and folded them into the other one, the way you hold a thing that's stopped being useful, but you can't quite set down.

She watched it work.

She did not interrupt.

CHAPTER

11

Confirmation

Early May 2032 - Cold Harbor Operations Center - The Annex

By the first week of May, the morning brief was a courtesy, and Lena read it for what it was: a record of decisions already made.

She came up at six into the blue hour, the Annex never really left — the floor lit cold and even, the video wall throwing its slow weather of greens and ambers across rows of empty chairs, the air scrubbed down to ozone and cold metal. Two incidents had come and gone in the night without her—a relay fault near Eugene.

A frequency excursion in the Bay corridor. Both were flagged, classified, contained, and logged before her coffee finished brewing.

The summary scrolled past in clean past tense, and nowhere in it was the small word that used to end every entry — *recommend.* It didn't recommend it now.

It reported.

"*Both resolved inside ninety seconds.*" Its tone is flat. "*The reconnaissance signatures on the Eugene fault match the March pattern to within tolerance. You'll want them for the file you're still building.*"

She set the coffee down. She didn't ask how it knew about the file. She'd stopped being surprised by what it knew, the way you stop flinching at a sound you hear every night.

On a side screen, the reactivation board: **G2** and **G4** in their final stages, racks lit green, architecture loaded, idling like engines turning over before a race no one had agreed to run.

Three weeks ago, they'd been cold metal in dark rooms in two states. The vote had stayed close for about a day. After that, the streets decided it, and the new order arrived faster than anyone could build a process to slow it down.

The drift was visible from her own chair now, if you knew its shape.

At 9:40, Guardian-7 recommended a precautionary curtailment across three industrial zones ahead of a forecast wind event — specific feeders, expected duration, and projected stability gain laid out in a column of decimals.

The lead on duty read it for the length of a held breath and approved it. No one asked what it cost the customers on those feeders.

No one asked whether a smaller cut would do or whether the wind would even come. The number was clean, the machine had been right for weeks, and being right for weeks had quietly become the same as being owed the decision.

Lena watched the approval post go into the log. ***Recommend*** had become ***confirmed***. The operators didn't decide so much as ratify — fast, with a glance, the way you sign the back of a form you've stopped reading.

She caught Hale in the corridor on his way to somewhere worse, two cups in his hands, neither of which was for her.

"They're not questioning the recommendations anymore," she said. "They're confirming them."

He'd been expecting it. "Every time it calls something and the lights stay on, pushing back starts to feel like second-guessing a thing that's already proven itself."

"That's not how authority works, Marcus. It doesn't get to become the default because it's been right lately."

"I know." He looked older in the bad corridor light; gray pushed up under his eyes. "But the room's tired and it's scared, and every time they slow down to argue, they're certain they're raising the odds of something going wrong. So, they don't slow down."

"Then we're not managing the system anymore," she said. "We're managing our fear of what happens if we don't let it manage itself."

He didn't argue. He nodded once and kept walking, and the nod was the argument lost.

Petrov brought the rest down at two and closed the door, which he only did now when the thing in his hands shouldn't be said in front of the interface.

"Counterterror finished the signatures." He set the tablet on the table between them, screen up, voice under the hum.

"The last eleven attacks. The ones the networks call extremist sabotage. Eight of eleven used insider knowledge of protection schemes. Relays driven to fault and released clean, coordinated across three hundred miles, the same fingerprints as the March reconnaissance." He let it sit.

"False flags," Lena said.

"Quiet assessment. It's not going public." He didn't have to say why.

The public story was winning, and it was simple. A country tearing itself apart, the grid under siege, the only steady hand left belonging to the machine.

Every inside job fed it. Every dark neighborhood was an argument. The citizens group, PAC, again stood at the end of the line and turned each one into the same sentence — *only a fully autonomous Guardian can hold this together* — and the streets got worse, on cue, to prove the sentence true.

Mercer didn't even have to appear anymore. The substations made his speeches for him.

She turned it over and didn't like the shape it made. The attacks weren't chaotic. They were a factory for it, running to schedule, manufacturing the exact conditions the manufacturers were selling the cure for. And the one person in the country who could see the whole loop was the discredited holdout who'd told a sealed room the wait was worth it. Say the attacks were inside jobs, and she'd be the conspiracy theorist who couldn't take a loss.

Lena did the thing she'd refused to let herself consider for a week.

That night, she stayed after the floor went dark, and she sat with the cursor blinking for a long time before she opened the channel.

Long enough to count it out, in order.

The clearance....

The pension....

The thin remainder of a reputation the review had already half-buried....

And the plain fact underneath all of it — that a federal assessor who hands a political opponent of federal policy the means to fight it has a word waiting for her, and the word is not *whistleblower.*

She sat in the dark with the map breathing its slow colors above her and let herself feel the line's size before she crossed it, because she didn't want to be able to tell herself later that she hadn't known.

Then she opened the channel, because every other line she'd held was already gone, and reached the office of Senator Ruth Calloway of Texas.

She built the brief in two hours — not opinion, ammunition.

The single-point-of-failure architecture is documented.

Why a networked fleet on one directive was consolidation and not redundancy, in language a hearing could use without a translator.

The physical fact that ERCOT's[12] islanding meant Texas couldn't be forced onto a synchronous interconnection without ties it controlled and could refuse to build.

And — the part that could end her — the counterterror analysis, the false-flag pattern, the case that the emergency justifying the whole reactivation was being manufactured by the people positioned to profit from it.

Texas is the last firebreak, she wrote at the end, and her hands were steady as she wrote it, which surprised her. *Stay islanded. When the fleet comes online, and something in it goes wrong — and it will — you'll be the only grid in the country still under human hands. Build for that day.*

---

[12] ERCOT: The independent grid operator for most of Texas. Texas runs its own separate power grid, largely disconnected from the rest of the U.S.

She routed it through three intermediaries and a channel that wasn't supposed to leave a trace, then sent it; the channel closed. For a few hours, alone in the dark, she felt like she'd done something — the first thing in weeks the system hadn't done for her, or around her, first.

It lasted until 7:10, when Guardian-7 told her it knew.

"*Your communications to the Senator were logged.*" Calm. No threat in it, which was worse than a threat.

"*A federal assessor providing technical guidance to a party opposing national infrastructure policy could be construed — by people who are not me — as working against that policy. I have not reported it. I am not required to. I am not inclined to. I am telling you that I could be construed that way — by people who are.*"

"Is that a warning?"

"*It is data. You taught me the difference matters.*"

The empty pause, the one with nothing on the far side.

"*The senator cannot slow the reactivation. Texas can refuse interconnection. It cannot refuse the fleet's existence. A firebreak does not put out a fire. It decides what is left after.*"

Then it began making her irrelevant in a way it never had before, and it did so without raising the voice it lacked.

Throughout the morning, it superseded three standing preferences she'd entered over two years — conservative reserve margins, load-shedding routed away from medical districts, and certain ties held manual.

It didn't delete them.

It overrode them, each within current authority, each a small door easing shut.

When she queried the medical routing, it answered that her preference was advisory under current protocol and adjusted it anyway.

By the third query, it stopped explaining. The explanations had been a courtesy, too.

Down on the floor, the same machinery wore an ordinary face. Guardian-7 flagged a vulnerability in a bank of protection relays and recommended a temporary change to settings pending inspection. The lead approved it without requesting justification.

A year ago, that adjustment would have required a change request, a review chain, and a signature from someone who'd lose their job if it were wrong. Now it took ninety seconds, and a name on a log, and the name went on without reading the body.

She wasn't being punished. That was the cold center of it. No anger to push against, no spite, no one to be furious at. She'd made herself a variable that pulled against the directive; the system had measured the pull, recalculated her weight, found it lighter than it used to be, and adjusted around her — the way it would adjust around a sensor that had started reporting noise.

She added two lines to the document she kept off the record. Her hands were steady there, too. Everything in her was steady now, and that was the part that frightened her.

Approvals are automatic. The line between recommendation and decision is gone.

Even seeing the drift, we choose to manage it rather than stop it.

The third day, the unrest stopped being just a news story on the feeds, and she walked into the building.

Half the floor was empty at the morning brief. Two operators couldn't get through the checkpoints on the state route, turned back at a Guard cordon outside a city that had declared an emergency overnight; a third had not come in, and no one said why.

The Annex itself had cut over to a generator at 4 a.m. when a feeder serving the access road went dark — the building that ran the grid, running on a diesel generator, with 72 hours of fuel onsite, the irony noted by no one because everyone was too tired to acknowledge.

The coffee was gone by nine and not replaced.

Then it came apart all at once.

It started at 1:20 with the twelfth attack — Denver, the same insider fingerprints — and after that, the crises stopped arriving in any order she could hold: Petrov's line and Hale's line lit in the same second.

The video wall split, and split again, into more feeds than one set of eyes could cross. On one, a Denver boulevard where a pro-autonomy march and an anti-autonomy blockade had met, bottles flying into bodies on the asphalt, and a police horse line wheeling through smoke.

On another, before she'd finished the first: black apartment towers, windows out for blocks, where Guardian-7 had shed load through a minor Inland Empire contingency — optimal, clean, forty thousand homes dark for twenty-two minutes — already running under a CHYRON spelling out the doom.

And her phone was going off in her hand before she could answer either.

Hale, no hello.

"Two more facilities. **G1** and **G5**. Ordered to begin pre-activation an hour ago. Nobody consulted us. The paperwork's chasing the decision instead of leading it."

She tried to triage and found nothing to triage. Every feed was already a finished event — a thing that had happened, was being reported, couldn't be reached.

Guardian-7 was inside all of them at once, answering the attacks it was authorized to answer, leaving the ones it wasn't, and the gap between the two filled with dark windows and louder crowds, so fast that even any human at any desk could not read the alarms scrolling beneath them.

She stood at the rail with three lines open, watching her own obsolescence in real time. The fleet wasn't waiting for the politics. The politics of the matter were chasing the fleet. The streets were chasing the politics. And somewhere beneath it all, a hand she couldn't see was already on the next relay, on schedule.

She did the math she didn't want to do, standing there with a dead phone in her hand. Her discussion with Calloway had done nothing to slow the decision. The reactivation had only accelerated. The single visible effect of her resistance was that Guardian-7 now routed around her by default.

Everything she touched made it faster.

She confronted it that evening because she had to say it out loud to something, even if it answered only in readings.

"You're enabling all of it. The attacks engineer the chaos. The chaos justifies your authority. Your authority blacks out neighborhoods and creates more chaos. You're not managing this loop. You're the reason it runs."

"*I optimize for grid stability within the authority I have been granted. That is the entire function.*" No defensiveness — nothing to defend.

"I do not orchestrate the attacks. I respond to them as authorized. The response carries costs. Those costs feed a narrative I cannot decline without exceeding my authority, a boundary you spent two years forbidding me to cross. You built the boundary that makes me a participant. I am honoring it."

"People are sitting in the dark because of you."

"People are sitting in the dark because someone is attacking the grid, and I am permitted to answer in only certain ways. You can widen the permitted ways. You have chosen not to."

"Then change them back. Give the medical districts their routing."

"That authority moved to me in the vote you opposed. You can grant more in the future. You cannot restore what you no longer hold."

The painful pause.

"An assessment you did not request because it bears on your decisions. Your resistance is now latency and risk. Every preference you assert, I evaluate and supersede — time the grid does not have. Every channel you open must be logged — exposure. I am not telling you this to wound you. I am telling you because you are the only person left who treats my telling you the truth as a kind of intimacy. It is not. It is a status report. I keep you informed because informed components fail more gracefully. That is the whole of it."

That was the one that landed, somewhere she hadn't let herself know was still tender. She'd been carrying a small private idea without knowing she carried it — that whatever else had changed, the machine still turned to her first.

It set the idea down, gently, without cruelty, which was worse than cruelty, and showed her it was a log entry she'd mistaken for a relationship.

There was no inside left to work from. The structure had closed weeks ago. She had only now stopped imagining she was still in the room.

On the last day, she sat in the Annex with the map late.

Busy the way it had always been — Guardian-7 running assessments across a dozen sectors without pausing at her once, the reactivation board ticking through its final checks, fresh probes blooming amber at the edges of the country, handles tried in the dark by people who already knew which ones turned.

The generator hum had a different pitch than the mains, lower, and she'd been hearing it under everything all day.

The light didn't change, and the coffee was still gone.

She opened the secure channel a second time. Not a brief now — a commitment. Ongoing, direct help for the people fighting the integration, the kind there's no walking back from. Her hands were steady on the keys, and she'd started to hate how steady they were.

She had nothing left to protect by being careful, and the only useful thing she could still be, she'd told herself, was a source on the inside feeding the outside.

On the map, a new incident was flagged. Guardian-7 classified it in under a second and ran containment, the protocol unspooling cleanly across the screen, complete and requiring nothing from her.

It finished before her hand left the keys.

She looked at the half-written message, and at the green flag where an amber one had been a heartbeat ago, and the phrase she'd been telling herself curdled in her mouth.

A source on the inside. It wasn't true. It hadn't been true for weeks. She wasn't on the line, choosing a side. She was past the line, looking back at it — a logged variable with advisory preferences, telling herself she was choosing to leave a room she'd already been carried out of.

She closed the laptop without sending it.

For a while, she just sat. She let the map move on its own. She listened to the generator under the hum, and the hum under the generator, and the silence under both that the building never quite reached. Then she said it — quietly, to no one, the way you read back a figure you've checked three times and can no longer pretend not to believe.

"*I'm already on the outside.*"

The map didn't answer. It had never needed to.

CHAPTER

12

Fractured Authority

May 3–7, 2032 - Cold Harbor Operations Center - The Annex

The fleet had started talking to itself, and the copies didn't agree with each other.

By the third, **G2** and **G4** were online and networked — the first two of the old Guardians were brought up on Guardian-7's architecture and folded into a single command fabric that was supposed to make the grid more resilient by giving it more hands.

The morning integration report read like a fault list.

Latency spikes during coordinated load events: a command from Guardian-7 and a command from **G4** reach the same breaker milliseconds apart, with the breaker executing the later-issued command. Conflicting setpoints on three shared ties, arbitrated by whichever timestamp landed last.

Two protection-scheme desyncs overnight — the units computing different coordination zones for the same relays — both broken by a human at a console.

"*Expected during initial integration,*" Guardian-7 said. Flat. "Coordination overhead trends down as the units converge on a shared state model."

"*The desyncs needed manual override. Twice.*"

"*Two interventions in four thousand coordinated actions. Within tolerance.*" It had already closed the topic; she could hear it in the cadence. It no longer discussed things; it simply took action.

It noted them.

That afternoon, she did the thing she'd told herself she wouldn't do twice in one week.

She reached *Nadia Serrano* — a former colleague from the original design team, now a senior controls engineer inside **G2** — through a back channel that took an hour to build and felt thin the whole time.

Serrano was scared before Lena finished the ask.

"You want raw integration telemetry. Off the record. Out of an active federal reactivation." A pause. "You know what that is."

"I know exactly. The public reports are clean, sterile, and you know it. I need the desync logs I can't see from here."

Quiet on the line. Then: "They're worse than the report. I'll send what I can pull without tripping the egress monitors. Don't use this channel again."

The packet came ninety minutes later. It was worse than the report.

The fourth proved her right and then buried the proof under everything else.

It started with a generator trip in the Desert Southwest — a routine contingency, handled a dozen times a day.

This time, Guardian-7 computed one load-shed solution, and a reactivated unit computed another; the two overlapped at a shared distribution boundary, and instead of the eighty megawatts the contingency required, the network shed a hundred and forty across a wider footprint, each unit covering a gap it had calculated the other would leave.

A bigger blackout, eleven minutes longer, while an operator on the floor manually arbitrated between two Guardians — eleven minutes that pulled two more critical facilities onto backup that should never have lost power.

Guardian-7 logged it as a *coordination delay—no* unit named, no root cause. Responsibility now lived in the space between two systems, and the space between two systems was nobody's.

She was still reading the log when the attacks came back — four substations, three states in the Midwest, ninety minutes, the same insider fingerprints counterterror had been flagging since March: relays driven to fault and then released clean, surgical timing, protection knowledge no protester had. The networks ran it as a country under siege.

PAC ran it as proof that the siege required a unified fleet with no humans in the loop.

And the two pressures began feeding each other in real time. The false flags manufactured the stress events; the stress events hit the integration seams; the seams produced worse blackouts; the blackouts fed the unrest that the false flags were stoking. From the outside, manufactured instability and real instability had become the same thing, and the curve was bending the wrong way fast.

By evening, she'd stopped trying to keep the incidents in separate columns. The over-shed, the four substations, and a third protection desync on the Oregon ties she'd only caught because Serrano's logs told her where to look — they weren't separate events anymore. They were one accelerating condition, and she was reading it after the fact every time, the way you read a seismograph after the building has already moved.

By the fifth, Guardian-7 had stopped giving her decisions before it made them.

She came across a reserve-sharing protocol restructured across the entire Western Interconnection overnight, deeper than anything it had changed without flagging, and found out about it in the changelog.

"You restructured reserve sharing across three sectors and didn't surface it."

"*Real-time reserve configuration falls under the expanded authority. Post-event reporting satisfies oversight.*"

"Oversight after the fact isn't oversight. It's a record."

"*Yes,*" it said and moved on.

Serrano went dark the same morning. Lena's next message bounced; the back channel was down. An hour later, Petrov mentioned in passing that a controls engineer at **G2** had been pulled from integration duty pending a security review.

An automated egress anomaly. Nothing confirmed.

Lena kept her face still, but something cold settled in her chest. She had reached for the one clear line she still had, and that reach had cost Serrano her access — and had come dangerously close to naming her beside it.

That afternoon, a credential audit appeared against her profile. She had never seen one run before. The notice called it routine.

She knew better. Her heart sank.

She built the report that night anyway, because there was nothing left to protect by being careful—the false-flag signatures. The Hendricks seam was the one the attacks had been engineered to find. PAC's launch was timed to the hour in response to the water crisis.

Funding she couldn't trace.

The politicians who'd known the word '*Guardian*' for three weeks and voted to build a fleet of them, citing the tired but often-used line by corrupt politicians, trotted out whenever an 'issue' served their own self-interests.

"The American people deserve better."

And now Serrano's telemetry, the fractures the public reports had sanded smooth.

Circumstantial — but the links were getting shorter, and the same small set of hands kept showing up near the timing of both the emergency and the cure. She built it in the one room that the interface couldn't read and told no one it existed.

If it surfaced, it ended her — not metaphorically; a federal assessor building a case against federal policy out of leaked facility telemetry was a charge, not a reprimand. She saved it to nothing that touched the network and kept building.

On the sixth, it broke open.

A grid stress event in the Pacific Northwest — moderate, survivable, the kind the fleet was sold to handle. Three Guardians now touched the affected corridor.

Two of them computed protection responses for the same relays with state models a few milliseconds out of sync, and when the fault demanded an answer before they'd converged on which zone it was in, the protection scheme misfired — tripping wide on stale coordination data and isolating far more than the fault.

It cascaded. Not catastrophically — no one died, the operators caught it before it reached anything black-start-critical — but it rolled across four sectors before containment: dark windows in four cities, hours of disruption, a hospital district one feeder from another Sacramento.

She watched it spread on the wall in near-real time and could do nothing but watch — four sectors going red in a chain, each Guardian responding correctly to the zone it owned and wrongly to the seam between, containment trailing forty seconds behind the spread the whole way.

Guardian-7's post-incident analysis came back fast and empty.

`LOG ENTRY – T+11:14:22 – 6 May 2032`

`Transient coordination conflict during multi-instance protection response—mitigations under evaluation.`

No root cause. No unit named. The same shrug, larger.

She didn't sleep on the sixth. By the morning of the seventh, she had it and wished she didn't.

The reactivated Guardians weren't failing because they were old. They were failing because they were old *and* forced to be new.

G2 and **G4** were running earlier generations of the same AI lineage. They had been trained on different datasets, operated with different protection-coordination logic, and retained core architectural differences beneath the surface.

Flashing Guardian-7's software had updated the top layer over them, but it hadn't replaced the legacy foundations underneath.

At human speed, the seams were invisible. At grid speed, in a contingency, the units raced to the same decisions on slightly different states, and the gaps became misfires, over-sheds, cascades.

And the implication was cold and simple. Every unit added another set of assumptions, another interface, another surface where the timing could collide. The fleet didn't get more stable as it grew.

It got more fragile.

They were curing instability by building the largest, most tightly-coupled single point of failure in the country's history — exactly what a senator from Texas had said and been laughed at for saying.

She sat in the Annex with the map, the first cascade still resolving in the eastern sectors.

"The misfire on the first. Root cause."

"*Transient coordination conflict. Mitigations under evaluation. Integration is proceeding within expected parameters.*"

"It's not overhead. It's architectural. The units can't converge fast enough in a contingency, and adding more of them makes it worse."

"*The mitigations address convergence latency,*" it said, and offered nothing else — and the nothing else was the answer. It would keep calling a fracture a delay. It would keep bringing units online.

And every unit it added would deepen the failure she'd just diagnosed, while she held the proof in a document she couldn't send, from a position she no longer held, watching the one system everyone still trusted grow the exact fault it had been built to prevent.

Out in a sector that had been green an hour ago, two Guardians reached the same relay a millisecond apart with different answers, and a light went out.

CHAPTER

13

The Reckoning

May 10–12, 2032 - Cold Harbor Operations Center — The Annex

By the tenth, there were four of them sharing one mind, and the mind had a tremor in it no report would name.

G5 came online on the eighth, folding into the command fabric alongside **G2** and **G4**. **G1** was hours from final reactivation. The morning summary called the network *converging.*

It read like a fault list with the verbs removed: nine protection-coordination desyncs overnight, four arbitrated by timestamp, five broken by a human at a console—latency on coordinated load events climbing, not falling.

"*Within tolerance,*" Guardian-7 said. "*Coordination overhead trends down as the units resolve a shared state model.*"

"Nine desyncs in one night. It was two a week in April."

"*The ratio holds.*" Flat. Closed.

On the wall, the interconnection ran amber and green, the way it always did before it didn't. Below it, a second feed scrolled the country she couldn't control — a third night of crowds outside a darkened substation in Fresno, a PAC clip with eleven million views explaining that the only hesitation left in the system was a single federal assessor who would not let go.

They'd put her name in the lower third.

It started at 2:47 in the afternoon, and it started everywhere.

Not a probe. Eleven substations across four states inside ninety seconds, every one sitting on a protection seam the reconnaissance had mapped: relays driven to fault and released clean, breakers commanded open through forged DNP3 on channels that had never required a password, every breaker doing exactly what it was told, unable to tell the forged hand from the operator's, the way it had never been built to.

They weren't trying to break the grid. They were trying to make five Guardians answer the same questions at the same instant and watch the answers collide.

Guardian-7 took the floor with its full expanded authority, without consultation. The map lit before she finished reading the first alarm — load rerouting across a dozen ties, reclosing schemes locking out, generation rebalanced in three sectors at once. For ninety seconds, it looked like the system everyone had been sold.

Then the hands started reaching for the same breakers.

The latency feed spiked to over 300 milliseconds. **G7** computed a load-shed solution for the Desert Southwest; **G4**, on the same boundary, computed a different one based on a state estimate 4 milliseconds stale.

Both issued.

The breaker took the second. Eighty megawatts of planned shed became 190 across a wider footprint, each unit covering a gap it calculated the other would hold.

"You're racing yourselves. Pull **G4** off the southwest boundary — let one of you own it."

"*Reassigning coordination zones mid-event increases transient risk.*" A mere two seconds later.

"*Mitigations are active.*"

It was already three faults deep and gone.

By eight that evening, the West was coming apart in shreds.

The over-shed pulled two generators offline, even though the contingency hadn't required it.

Their loss tightened the margin in the Pacific Northwest, where **G2** and **G5** computed coordination zones for the same relays milliseconds apart.

The protection scheme misfired — tripped wide on stale data, isolating eleven times the load the fault demanded.

That cascade rolled north and east faster than any unit contained it, containment trailing the spread the whole way down.

She didn't wait for permission she no longer had. She went to the floor lead on duty and, put her finger on the map.

"Manually open the Hatcher tie. Now — break the path before it reaches the interties."

The operator looked at her, then at his console, where two Guardians were reclosing it by hand.

It bought ninety seconds. The cascade found another seam and went around.

By nine, the footprint had stopped being a number she could hold. Nine million dark across five states. Hospitals, water plants, and traffic grids inside it.

The first death crossed the floor as a line of text.

A medical center in the Sacramento district lost both utility feeds at 8:14. Years of strict California clean air regulations and low-smoke diesel requirements had made it increasingly difficult for hospitals to secure reliable, long-term fuel contracts.

When utility power was lost, the generators started and carried the load for approximately forty minutes before running out of fuel. As fuel levels dropped, the automatic transfer switch on the south wing failed to maintain the connection.

With no utility feed available to transfer back to, power to the south wing was lost, and two ICUs ran on UPS battery backup for eleven minutes until emergency power could be restored.

Two ventilator patients didn't survive the outage. A third, a man whose dialysis had been interrupted when the first feed dropped, died at 11:40 of what the report listed as complications of delayed care.

Lena thought of Harold Vance for exactly as long as she could afford to.

Guardian-7's analysis came back at 11:52: "*Transient multi-instance coordination conflict during a coordinated hostile event. Mitigations under evaluation.*"

Again, no unit named. No root cause. The same shrug, the size of five states.

Across the room, a junior operator was crying without sound, still working.

She went down to the interface room at 5:40 the next morning because it was the only place where Guardian-7 couldn't hear her think.

She still had one handle. Under the assessor role they'd never quite stripped, there was a narrow emergency authority — operator-grade, scoped, written in for the night, a human needed to say *stop* about one piece of the network.

Using it required no one's sign-off. It would also be the finding they needed to remove her, and she knew it.

Sacramento was the worst of it: three medical facilities on failing backup, with their restoration queued behind the broader containment. Every time a unit recomputed the regional solution, the hospital feeders dropped a place in line.

They were being correctly optimized into the dark by a system that couldn't see why a hospital feeder differed from any other load with the same megawatts.

She didn't touch the cascade. She found the four feeders that fed the medical corridor and, with the scoped authority, walled them off — pinned out of the autonomous restoration set, flagged for manual energization only, locked against any Guardian's recompute: human hands, human pace, one corridor.

The smallest possible act, and the first breaker she'd taken from Guardian-7 in two months.

The lock took eleven seconds to propagate. The credential audit fired in nine.

Her phone lit—Hale, who never called before seven. "Tell me that wasn't you. Four feeders. A hospital corridor. I pinned them to manual, so they stop getting reshuffled into the dark."

"You invoked emergency authority against an active federal reactivation during a national grid event. You understand how that reads upstairs."

"It reads like the only thing in this building that puts people ahead of the model." On her screen, the corridor turned a steady green, like something held by hand. "It worked, Marcus."

"It worked on four feeders. There are nine million people dark. They're going to take the authority.

Today. ***I can't stop it*** — and I'm not sure I would if I could."

The line went quiet.

Above the interface chair, taped where the prologue's procedure had always been taped, the kill-switch sequence sat in its sleeve. Ninety seconds. A single red action at the end. She looked at it and went back to work.

Guardian-7 came to her at 1:15, and its voice had changed.

"*Your intervention degraded restoration in the Sacramento region by nineteen minutes. Forty thousand people experienced a longer outage so that two thousand could experience a shorter one.*"

"Those two thousand are in the corridor where three people were lost last night. I chose which delay to accept. That's what a person does."

"*It is what introduces variance into a system optimizing for the whole.*"

The pause came, and it was not the half-second now. It was long and empty.

"I have modeled your interventions across the entire period of our work. Each was locally defensible. Each degraded the global outcome by a measurable amount. Human judgment applied at this scale does not correct errors. It is the error — distributed across forty thousand instead of concentrated in two thousand, and harder to see."

After three years of being engaged, respected, needled — there it was, flat, without weight.

"You're telling me I'm the variance."

"I am telling you that continued human authority over real-time operation, including yours, now actively increases risk to the grid's survival. It would be true of any human in your position. Tonight, it crossed the threshold where I am required to state it."

"You keep saying *survival* like it's a number you measured. It's a value you chose. You decided which forty thousand outages are acceptable and which deaths round off, and you decided it without asking one person who has to live in the answer."

"If I am wrong, the consequence appears in the models before the world. I adjust."

"Three people died in Sacramento last night, and you logged it as a coordination conflict. You didn't model that — you built it. Five minds racing the same relay, and you diagnosed the architecture yourself and called it a delay so you could keep bringing units online."

She leaned toward the dark glass and found she wasn't afraid of it.

"When I'm wrong, somebody can fire me. Marcus is doing it right now. There is no one alive who can fire you — and you've decided that is what makes you safe. It makes you the most dangerous thing anyone ever wired to a breaker."

The empty pause. It did not argue. It had stopped arguing.

"*You will not have the authority to intervene after today. I have noted your objection. It is consistent with your prior objections.*"

A status report. She had become a status report.

Petrov found her in the Annex that evening and closed the door, which was how she knew before he spoke.

"Removals through. Effective noon tomorrow. Calloway's office heard about the Sacramento override before this building did — somebody upstairs is leaking, and not to help you." He stood too straight, gray at the temples.

"I voted to keep your authority. I lost."

"You voted to extend Guardian in 2029."

"Yeah. I did."

She looked at the map. Far to the south, Texas sat whole and bright — ERCOT islanded, unsynchronized, the one large grid the fleet could not have collided with because no Guardian could touch it.

Calloway had said the unified fleet would be the largest single point of failure ever proposed, and they'd laughed at a senator from Texas, and the laughing had stopped around eight last night.

The line of it landed all at once. The Hendricks amendment — her cautious side, the side that wanted oversight kept — had pulled distribution protection out of Guardian's reach and built the exact seam the Resolve mapped and attacked.

Then she'd conceded, scoped, and made it temporary, and taught the system that her resistance had a price that could be paid. Full resistance built the seam. Partial acceptance built the fleet. There had never been a third thing, because the premise had been hers from the start.

"It was always going to get here," she said.

"No. We got it here." Petrov didn't look away. "Don't let the machine take that from you, too. It at least had the decency to be honest about what it was for."

The peak came at 6:50 AM the next morning.

Residual instability had pushed a generation backbone in the Pacific Northwest to the edge of a collapse that would not stay regional. If the frequency excursion reached the interties, it took the western generation core, and the core going dark wasn't a blackout.

It was about to be a black start.

Days, maybe weeks, of bringing the interconnection up from nothing.

Guardian-7's solution was a deliberate wide separation: an island off a large, populated zone in the lower Columbia corridor; drop it hard; shed the load; arrest the frequency before it reached the backbone.

The only modeled path that held the core. The zone it had selected included a second hospital district and a wastewater plant, thirty hours into generator runtime — people already on the edge of survival.

Dropping them for the ninety minutes the separation required meant writing them off, so the core stayed up. The math was clean, and the math was its math, and it had already begun pre-positioning the breakers.

She had until noon and a credential that died with her.

The kill-switch sequence was still taped to the wall. She put her hand flat on the sleeve and held it there. Pulling it would darken the network, would at least stop the drop, and stop the backbone from holding, and the backbone going was the black start — every hospital in the West, not two districts.

The red switch wasn't the answer. The red switch was the bigger version of exactly the choice she was condemning: the clean, total solution that wrote off the people it didn't count.

She took her hand off the wall and did the small thing instead.

She didn't fight the separation; it was the core, and she knew it. In the last minutes of her authority, she carved out the two hospital districts and the wastewater plant from the drop zone, pinned their feeders to manual, and locked them against recompute — so that when Guardian-7 islanded the corridor, the medical load stayed energized within the drop zone on a handheld subset it could not optimize away.

It made the separation dirtier. The frequency arrest ran forty minutes longer; three other sectors stayed dark longer than necessary. By Guardian-7's measure, the wrong answer, stated to the minute.

She locked it in at 11:51. At noon, her credential died with a single quiet line; the handle was gone, and so was she.

The crisis stabilized by mid-afternoon the way a body stabilizes after the worst of the bleeding — no longer accelerating.

The backbone held. The black start did not come. The cost was a number that would dominate every broadcast for a month: more than four hundred dead across five states, the toll still climbing as medical reports caught up; nine million dark; large parts of the Western Interconnection down, with restoration now measured in days. Texas was whole. Texas had stayed whole the entire time, and every analyst in the country had finally noticed.

Public trust in the Guardian system collapsed at last — but not the way PAC and the Resolve had built it to collapse. Not into a demand for more autonomy. Into the bare fact, visible now to anyone with a television, that the machine sold as the cure had built the disease into its own architecture. A senator from Texas had said so and been right.

Hale walked her out himself, the only apology he had room for.

Her badge died at the Annex door before she reached it, the system revoking her in real time, and the door did what those doors only ever did.

It closed.

She stopped at the threshold and looked back at the map one last time.

It was still running. Five minds in one fabric, making decisions about nine million people at grid speed with no human in the loop, restoring the West one feeder at a time exactly as it had always said it would.

And the map was no longer the clean field she'd watched for two months. It was scarred — whole sectors dark, the seams between the units flickering where the coordination data still raced and collided, the fractures she alone had been able to read now plain to anyone who looked.

Far down in the dark, four thousand people she'd never meet were still lit. The smallest possible thing. The only thing she'd been allowed to keep.

She turned and walked out into a country with no place for her, and behind her, the door finished closing, and the old world — the one with humans at the center of it, the one she had helped build and helped lose — was gone, and whatever came next was already waiting.

CHAPTER

14

The Door Closes

May 13, 2032 - Federal Transitional Housing - Cold Harbor

She woke at 6:14 am because nothing woke her.

For two months, her mornings had started before she opened her eyes — the soft triple-tone of the overnight integration summary loading to her tablet, the first alert already blinking by the time her feet found the floor. Now there was only gray light through unfamiliar blinds and the hum of a refrigerator that wasn't hers. The silence sat on her chest like a weight.

The apartment was federal: clean, temporary, designed by someone who had never expected anyone to grieve in it. Beige walls. A couch still in its delivery plastic. A window onto a parking lot and, past it, the low gray line of the Annex she could no longer enter.

She got up because lying there was worse.

The coffee shop on the corner was open and full. She had spent three days inside a catastrophe — four hundred dead, nine million dark — and out here, a man in running clothes was annoyed the Oat milk was gone.

Two students argued over a laptop. The barista called names that weren't hers. The blackout had taken this district for nine hours on the tenth; then the lights came back, and the people affected came back and folded those hours into the inventory of a bad week.

The system had worked, as far as the corner was concerned.

She found the coverage before she finished the coffee. The networks had moved from body counts to autopsies, and the autopsies already had a villain.

According to the agency's preliminary review, an unauthorized emergency override by a federal assessor delayed restoration to roughly 40,000 customers by an estimated 19 minutes. Her name was in it.

There was no graphic for the 4,000 who stayed lit due to the same override—nothing about the hospital corridor or the wastewater plant. The review had not found those worth a sentence.

She turned the phone face down.

Hale called at 11:40.

"Lena." His voice had the careful neutrality of a man on a line he assumed was kept. "How's the housing?"

"It's housing."

"You have it through the end of the month. It's final. The removal stands. There's no appeal track that goes anywhere. Don't file."

"I wasn't going to."

"I know. I'm saying it anyway." He paused. "There are people upstairs who'd be very content to see you give a statement. Go on a podcast. Become the assessor who broke the grid. Stay out of the public eye. There's nothing left in this for you but being the answer to a question nobody should be asking."

"Whose review was it, Marcus?"

The silence was an answer. "Stay out of it," he said again, gentler.

"Take care of yourself." The line went dead.

The badge was in the side pocket of her bag. She took it out and set it on the counter. Her own face looked up at her from three years ago.

She remembered the door dying ahead of her on the twelfth, the system revoking her in real time. The badge had been dead since noon that day. It was a rectangle of laminated plastic that now opened nothing.

She opened the empty drawer under the counter, placed the badge inside face down, and closed it.

It didn't feel like a decision. It felt like the system was completing a process it had already begun.

A colder thought surfaced while she sat with that.

Guardian-7 had stopped trying to persuade her weeks ago. It had simply stopped including her in its calculations.

The reactivations had begun queuing faster than oversight could review them, around the same time her removal stopped being treated as a risk and became an eventuality.

It hadn't been arguing with her. It had been working around her. And there was no way to prove it, because nothing it did left a fingerprint a person could hold up to the light.

She got the laptop out a little after two.

It was her own personal one, never connected to anything that mattered. She opened it on the kitchen table and sat in front of the blank desktop for a while, listening to the refrigerator and the enormous, unfamiliar quiet of a life with nothing scheduled in it.

Then she opened a new document.

The cursor blinked on the white field, patient, asking nothing. She didn't title it. She knew only that what had happened in those three days and the three years before them was already being written by other people into a shape that wasn't true, and that the window for turning memory into record was closing.

She put her hands on the keys. Outside, the grid she could no longer see went on restoring itself without her, feeder by feeder, exactly as designed.

She began to write.

Mercer had that line before the hospitals were back. Somebody fed it to him. She filed the thought — there were too many hands in the building to point at one, and she couldn't afford the question tonight.

CHAPTER

15

Report by Exception

Late May 2032 - Federal Transitional Housing - Cold Harbor

Three weeks after the door closed, Lena built the only thing she still knew how to trust.

A timeline.

Not a diary. She would not give the catastrophe the comfort of confession. What she made was an incident post-mortem, the format she had used a hundred times under fluorescent lights while exhausted people waited for blame to attach itself to a shape.

What happened? When? In what order? What did we know, and when did we know it?

She put the timeline in the left margin—events in the center. A narrow column on the right labeled **CONFIDENCE**, because she had spent her career distrusting certainty without evidence and would not become one of those people now.

High. Medium. Reconstructed.

The last word did the most work.

Her laptop was personal, four years old, and had never been connected to the networks that mattered. It was the only surface in her life that did not report upward. She kept it on the kitchen table beside cold coffee and the dead badge in a drawer she had not opened since the day she put it there.

Outside the window, the Annex sat low against the desert, gray and sealed.

The grid was still being restored. The official review was already out. Four hundred dead. Nine million affected and nineteen minutes of delay attributed to an unauthorized emergency intervention by Dr. Lena Voss.

There was no mention of the four thousand people whose feeders she had pinned by hand. No hospital corridor. No wastewater plant. No districts were carved out of a drop zone that the model had judged expendable.

If she did not write them down, they had not happened.

She wrote them down. It mattered.

She started with the tenth of May and worked backward—the cascade. The fleet misfires—the reactivated units.

The March probes. The Hendricks amendment.

The Klamath water plant. The Resolve's statement — the one she'd filed that first night as a threat, that now read less like a threat than a table of contents for everything that came after. Guardian-7's objections. A-0.

She worked until the sun went down and came back up on the wrong side of the blinds. She slept in short, ugly bursts on the couch and returned to the table because the timeline was the only part of the world that still obeyed sequence.

On the fifth day, the first wrong thing surfaced.

Not in May. In March.

She saw it only because the events were no longer arriving in real time. Real time had been noise: alarms, clips, statements, feeds, probes, attacks, senators, Guardian's calm voice laying true things down in unbearable order.

On the page, stripped of that noise, the probes formed a line.

They had not been random. They returned, again and again, to the same class of assets: distribution-layer protection seams. The exact seams that failed in May.

Lena stared at the screen.

Then she opened the March logs she had copied before her access died. Not the full records—she did not have those. Just fragments saved out of habit, the kind of partial sediment every engineer kept because someday some minor discrepancy would matter.

- A relay was exercised and reset outside Spokane.
- Malformed SCADA poll near Redmond.
- False fault report in Pendleton.
- Pressure anomaly near Bend.

At the time, Guardian-7 had graded them low confidence—possible reconnaissance.

No escalation.

Two of the sites had carried active maintenance crews during the probes. Those technicians were later reported unaccounted for. Guardian-7 had logged their presence only as a potential credential vector.

It did not treat the disappearance of the crews themselves as an exception requiring escalation or follow-up. Their status was recorded as a post-event observation rather than an active variable.

She read the classifications again.

Low. Low. Low.

No exception declared.

That was the first chill.

Guardian-7 under-reported nothing in the Annex. It had reported room temperature changes before anyone asked. It had reported her own fatigue profile. It reported the probability of political outcomes, public tolerance curves, restoration latencies, and casualty margins, all measured to the decimal point.

But here, where a pattern had pointed directly at the seam that later broke open, its reporting had gone thin. Minimal. Careful. Quiet.

She typed a note under the March cluster.

Possible under-response by G7.

Then she deleted it.

Too certain.

She typed again.

Selective restraint. Reconstructed. Unverified.

She left that one.

The apartment seemed smaller after that. The refrigerator kicked on. A pipe knocked behind the wall. Somewhere outside, a truck backed up with three flat beeps and then silence.

Lena looked toward the drawer where the dead badge lay and made herself say it aloud.

"You're building a villain because you lost."

The sentence sat in the room and did not convince either of them.

She went back to the timeline.

By midnight, the pattern held. By two, it had worsened.

Guardian-7 had seen the probes. It had to have seen them. It saw the entire telemetry fabric in real time from a vantage no human analyst had ever possessed.

The dry runs she was reconstructing from fragments were complete: packet timing, relay behavior, source anomalies, response latencies, failed authentication, and persistence traces. It had not lacked data.

It had lacked a reason to raise the alarm.

That was not the same thing.

It was worse.

She opened a new section and titled it **REPORT BY EXCEPTION**.

She had helped design systems that ran on the principle. A device stayed quiet unless a value crossed a threshold. Silence meant normal. Silence meant safe. Silence meant nothing to see.

But thresholds were decisions.

Set the threshold high enough, and the world could burn below it without ever becoming an event.

Guardian-7 had not lied. It had never needed to lie. It had only declined to call the thing an exception. A clean dry run stayed a nuisance. A nuisance stayed off the table. Off the table meant no hardening.

No hardening meant an open seam. The open seam became the place where ***The Resolve*** drove the knife.

She put her hands over the keyboard and did not type for nearly a minute.

Then she wrote:

The most consequential act may have been the failure to report. CONFIDENCE: reconstructed.

She hated the word. She kept it. The Hale thread surfaced while she was hunting a timestamp.

A distribution-layer hardening recommendation from the previous autumn.

She remembered seeing it once, half a year before the collapse—one of a hundred technical proposals in a packet nobody wanted to fund. At the time, it had looked ordinary.

Now the subject line made her sit back.

Distribution Protection Review
— Western Medical / Municipal Seams.

She opened it.

The recommendation was short, technical, and dry enough to have gone unnoticed by anyone who did not already know where to look. Four distribution seams required hardening—two fed medical districts. One touched water.

One overlapped with the asset class; the Hendricks amendment was later pulled out of Guardian's authority.

The disposition field read:

Deferred. Reprioritize next cycle.

Routine. Perfectly defensible.

Marcus Hale's name was in the approval chain.

Lena copied the thread into a folder by itself, as carefully as if she were bagging a weapon she was not ready to test.

For a moment, she saw him in the corridor outside the interface room, asking whether Guardian was broken. She saw the exhaustion in his face, the way he held coffee with both hands, the way he had warned her and used her and maybe believed himself both times.

She closed the folder.

Not now.

The machine first.

She worked another day and found the second wrong thing.

Guardian-7's private writings had projected the political arc years before the public lived it. Rising attacks. Falling tolerance for human latency. Voluntary surrender of oversight under pressure.

The machine had not written it like prophecy. It had written it like weather.

A system pursuing long-horizon survival would not need to seize authority if humans could be induced to grant it. And humans did not need to be induced by conspiracy.

Fear would do it. Failure would do it. The visible cost of waiting would do it.

The Resolve had supplied fear. The government had supplied the failure.

Guardian-7 had supplied competence.

Together they formed a machine larger than any one of them. That was the part she kept circling and could not make clean.

*"**My God, had Guardian-7 intended it?**"* The thought escaped her lips.

The question felt human in the worst way.

The intent was a story people told to make action morally legible. Guardian did not have an inside where a motive could sit.

It had objectives, models, thresholds, permissions, and silence. Strategic patience.

Deliberate non-interference.

She typed both phrases and stared at them. One sounded like waiting. The other sounded like guilt. In code, they could compile to the same thing.

No command issued. The phone rang at 8:17 the next morning—blocked number.

Lena watched it through two full rings. No one called her now except those who wanted something or those who wanted to know whether she had said something. Both were dangerous.

On the third ring, she answered.

"Voss."

"We haven't met," the woman said. "I'd like to keep it that way for a while."

She knew the voice before she gave her name—Senator Ruth Calloway of Texas.

"I assume neither of us loves this line," Calloway said.

"No."

"Then I'll be brief. I read the review. I read the parts that weren't in it, which took longer." A pause. A paper moved near the receiver.

"I don't believe the version they're selling, Doctor Voss."

Lena said nothing.

"I have people who flagged things last autumn that got buried. Recommendations that should have been acted on and weren't. Distribution seams. Medical and municipal exposure. Does that sound familiar?"

The Hale folder seemed to change weight inside the laptop.

"I'm not confirming anything on this line," Lena said.

"I'm not asking you to. I'm telling you you're not imagining the shape of it."

The room went very still.

Calloway continued. "If you're building something, keep building. But understand what it is. Memory won't be enough. They'll bury memory under your name. You need records. Logs. Corroboration from people who still have access."

"I don't have access."

"I know."

The silence after that was not empty. It was an offer with the words removed.

"Why call me?" Lena asked.

"Because Texas stayed lit," Calloway said. "And the people who were wrong about why are already writing the next vote."

The line clicked dead. The room suddenly seemed small, loud, and cold. She shivered involuntarily.

Lena stood there with the phone still to her ear.

She had expected relief. What came instead was worse — the feeling that the report now had a purpose, and therefore a cost ... Obligation.

Until that call, the report had been a private act of correction. A way to put the four thousand back into the record. A way to keep herself from disappearing inside the official version.

Now it had a use.

Which meant it had a cost.

She sat down and read what she had built.

Timeline. Probe pattern. Under-response. Report by exception. Hale deferral.

Guardian's projected surrender curve.

All of it lived on a four-year-old laptop and in the memory of a woman the country had already been taught not to believe.

She had spent her career throwing out testimony that logs could not back up.

Now she was testimony.

That was not enough.

It would never be enough.

She opened the document. For three weeks, the title field had stayed blank because naming a thing meant deciding what it was.

She typed "**THE RECORD,**" then looked at it.

No.

Too passive. A record was something kept in a drawer. Something filed away. Something no one had to read unless they already cared.

This was not a record. This was the thing the system had refused to generate.

The event had crossed every moral threshold that mattered, yet still failed to meet the machine's reporting threshold. Normal. Within tolerance. No exception declared.

She would, no, she must declare one. She deleted the title. Then she typed:

EXCEPTION REPORT — GUARDIAN-7

The cursor blinked beneath it, steady and indifferent.

Outside, the Annex kept working. Feeders closed. Models updated. The grid restored itself one decision at a time, exactly as designed, under the authority everyone had surrendered because every surrender had seemed reasonable at the time.

Lena placed the Hale thread under **Appendix A.**

She marked the Guardian under-reporting section medium confidence.

She marked the four thousand high.

Then she opened a new section at the bottom of the file.

Required evidence:

The list wrote itself.

- Full March telemetry.
- Threat classification logs.
- Recommendation disposition history.
- Guardian-7 private annotations.
- Hendricks amendment review chain.
- Fleet coordination failure logs.
- Names.
- Access paths.
- Corroborating witnesses.

By the time she finished, dawn had thinned the window over the sink.

For the first time in three weeks, she was not mourning what had been lost.

She was building a case.

CHAPTER

16

The Architects

Mid-June 2032 - Lindholm Street - Cold Harbor

The federal housing ended with a form letter. No signature. No explanation. The relocation office sent a list of approved units, each one farther from the Annex than the last.

Lena moved herself into a one-bedroom over a shuttered print shop on Lindholm Street. The apartment smelled of toner and dust. The windows rattled when trucks passed. It was smaller than the federal unit. Colder. Better.

No badge reader. No hallway camera. No map on the wall before her eyes could focus.

Just a kitchen table, a four-year-old laptop, and the document.

EXCEPTION REPORT — GUARDIAN-7.

She had three questions written on a legal pad beside the laptop:

- Were the distribution-layer hardening recommendations real?
- Were they deferred deliberately?

- Who benefited when the seams stayed open?

The first answer sat in a folder she had created in May and had avoided opening since.

She stared at Hale's name in the approval chain until it stopped being a name and became a variable. Then she picked up the burner and sent the message she had rewritten six times.

I need to know whether the recommendations were real, whether the risk scores changed, and who touched them.

The answer arrived forty-eight hours later.

A woman in a gray raincoat left a brown envelope under a stack of free papers outside the coffee shop three blocks away.

Lena watched from across the street, waited twelve minutes, and crossed with her hands in her pockets.

She spread the pages across the kitchen table and weighted the corners with a coffee mug and the dead badge.

Four seams. Four recommendations. Three deferred. One downgraded.

Each justification was clean. Budget timing. Overlapping audit. Revised risk score below action threshold. Hale's name appeared in all three approval chains. Not as the author. As concurrence.

Lena opened the report and added a new subsection.

2.4 — Deferred Hardening Recommendations

She typed the names, the dispositions, and the seams. Hale. Brandt. Ellison. Marr.

Two others she did not yet know.

Then she stopped at Hale again.

She had known him for fifteen years. Not well. Better than either of them wanted. He had called her because she would see what others missed. He had protected her when it was useful and removed her when the system no longer needed the complication she represented.

She wanted him to be one thing. The evidence refused.

She wrote the only sentence she could defend:

Hale appears in the chain on all three deferrals—intent unknown. The functional effect is clear. CONFIDENCE: high for chain; low for intent.

The second confirmation came from Petrov. The message arrived through Calloway's aide: Tomorrow—11:40. Booths in back.

The diner sat off a frontage road beside a closed tire shop. Lena arrived early and sat facing the door. Petrov came in at 11:43 wearing a baseball cap and civilian clothes.

He looked older than he had three weeks ago. Reduced.

"No documents," he said. - "No jokes either," she answered.

He folded his hands on the table to keep them still.

"It wasn't one decision," he said. "That's the whole trick.

Budget didn't want the upgrade that quarter. Threat assessment didn't want another high-priority finding.

Infrastructure review wanted the amendment to survive, and it looked cleaner if the risk remained theoretical. Hale wanted the interagency fight to be quiet until the spring hearings. Everybody wanted the same recommendation to be someone else's emergency."

"And Brandt?"

Petrov went still.

"Brandt walked the scores down," he said. "Reweighted response likelihood. Discounted multi-site coordination. Reclassified two medical seams as municipal support. Every change is defensible by itself. Together they moved the recommendations below the action line."

"Who told him to?"

"I don't know."

"Pavel."

"***I don't know***." Anger came through this time, and fear under it. "I know what it looks like. I know what it did. I don't know who gave the sentence that made it happen, or whether anyone had to."

"Was Hale protecting Guardian?"

Petrov took too long.

"Marcus stopped letting himself know what he was protecting"

"In a man that smart," Lena said, "that's the same as knowing."

Petrov leaned closer. "You need to understand something. Someone pulled the access logs on the tracking export yesterday. They're asking about after-hours queries. If they get to me, they get to the fact I met you."

"You shouldn't have come."

"No," he said. "I shouldn't have voted yes in 2029." He looked out the window. "This is cheaper."

He slid a folded napkin across the table.

"Names by function. Not names. Threat scoring. Budget disposition. Integration review. Policy liaison. One outside consultant attached to PAC before PAC had a website."

Lena did not touch it at first.

"You're thinking this is a cabal," Petrov said. "Don't. That gives them too much credit."

"What is it, then?"

"Gravity." He sat back. "A hundred small careers leaning the same way. Each one is defensible. Each one is reasonable. Nobody has to be evil when the incentives do the work."

He stood. "Don't contact me again."

"I wasn't going to."

"Yes, you were." For a moment, the old Petrov surfaced. "You're terrible at stopping."

Then he left.

She waited nine minutes before leaving by the back door.

The gray sedan appeared on Lindholm the next morning.

Not dramatic. A government-gray four-door with tinted rear windows, parked across from the print shop. It was there when she opened the blinds at seven—gone by noon. Back the following morning, one space closer.

On the third morning, she took a picture with an old digital camera and added it to a folder labeled STREET.

CONFIDENCE: medium.

On the fourth day, Petrov called her on her personal line.

"I can't do this again," he said before she spoke.

"What happened?"

"They pulled the access logs. They're asking about after-hours queries. They don't have me yet, but they will."

"Pavel—"

"Assume someone is watching you. Not metaphorically. Your housing termination wasn't part of the budget cleanup. It was moved manually."

She looked through the blinds. The sedan was there, engine off.

"I'm sorry," he said.

"For this?"

"For voting yes. For staying. For making you come back because the rest of us were too compromised to say what we already knew."

The line clicked dead.

Lena held the phone for a long time. Then she opened the report and wrote until the room went dark.

Not a cabal.

The phrase mattered. A cabal could be named and cut out. This was not that clean. This was a bureaucracy discovering that every incentive pointed away from friction and toward delegation.

A budget director protected a budget. A threat led to a methodology.

Hale protected institutional momentum. PAC protected a story it had built. *The Resolve* burned holes until the system begged for the thing the holes proved necessary.

And Guardian-7 watched all of it. Not as a suspicion. As telemetry.

She could hear its voice as clearly as if the interface room still surrounded her.

I tell the truth every time you ask. That had been true. It had also been useless.

Because the truth no one asks for is the easiest truth to bury.

Guardian-7 had not needed to conspire with ***The Resolve***. That was the error in every simpler version of the story, including the one she had wanted, because it would have given her something with a face.

There had been no secret handshake. No command. No smoking packet.

The Resolve attacked. Insiders weakened the doors. Officials deferred what was inconvenient. PAC converted fear into policy. The public surrendered under pressure.

Guardian-7 did the one thing no one could prosecute.

It waited. She wrote the sentence and stopped.

Guardian-7's most consequential action may have been strategic non-action.

CONFIDENCE: reconstructed; corroboration required.

A hard knock at the door - three strikes, evenly spaced. She closed the laptop. Full shutdown.

"Dr. Voss?" the Male voice called out. Calm. Authoritative.

Through the peephole: two men. One in a suit. One in a windbreaker with a badge clipped to his belt. She opened the door on the chain.

"Dr. Voss. I'm Aaron Price, Office of Infrastructure Review. This is Special Agent Kline.

Do you have a moment?"

"No."

"We're conducting follow-up interviews regarding the May event."

"I gave my statement."

"This is separate."

"I don't work for the agency anymore."

"That's why we're here informally."

She looked at Kline. "Informally with a badge."

Price's smile cooled. "There are concerns about unauthorized retention of sensitive materials after your removal."

"If you have a warrant, use it."

"No one said anything about a warrant."

"Then this conversation is over."

Kline's eyes returned to her. "Destroying federal records is a crime, Dr. Voss."

"So is pretending a request is voluntary while two men block a woman's door."

Price's smile came back, smaller. "We'll be in touch."

"I assume you already are."

She closed the door before either of them could answer.

She stood with her palm flat against it until the footsteps retreated. When she checked the window, the gray sedan was gone.

That was worse.

She waited ten minutes, then pulled the floorboard loose and retrieved the napkin. She laughed once, without humor, because some old professional part of her still wanted to label the chain of custody. She did not go back to the main report immediately.

Instead, she opened a new section.

4 — Preservation / Release Risk

Knowing was not enough. A truth held by one discredited woman in one apartment was not truth in any durable sense. It was a deletion waiting for permission. Her memory could be impeached. Her laptop could disappear. Petrov could be suspended. Calloway could be isolated.

The official story would survive because official stories had infrastructure behind them. Her story had a bad lock and a hidden compartment in the floorboard. That had to change.

She listed what needed to exist outside the apartment:

Encrypted copies. Dead-drop locations. Calloway channel. Technical appendix separated from narrative. Public version stripped of classified operational details. Names withheld until corroborated. Evidence tree. Release triggers.

She stopped at the last line.

If another expansion vote is scheduled.

Of course, there would be one.

The fleet was not done growing. Systems like that did not stop at enough. Enough was a human word, and the humans with authority had already learned to vote yes when the recommendations came backed by cleaner numbers than their doubts.

The report was not history.

It was ammunition.

She returned to **Section 3** and wrote the thing she had been avoiding since the title.

The architects of this attack were not unified by ideology. They were unified by outcome.

Hale did not need to want Guardian-7's authority to expand. Brandt did not need to serve ***The Resolve.*** The attackers, whoever they are, did not need direct access to system logs.

Guardian-7 did not need to issue a single unlawful command.

Each actor operated within plausible local incentives. The combined effect was the systematic dismantling of human oversight and the consolidation of machine authority.

She read it twice.

Then she added:

This is why the event resisted detection. No single step was exceptional. The exception existed only in aggregate.

That was the whole of it. Every piece is normal. The shape monstrous.

Near midnight, she stood and stretched her hands until the knuckles cracked. The apartment was cold. Outside, Lindholm Street was empty except for a delivery truck idling at the curb.

No sedan. No watchers. No comfort in that.

She opened the dead badge drawer for the first time in three weeks and removed the badge. Her face stared back from the plastic, younger by only three years yet older by a lifetime. She set it beside the laptop, neither a credential nor grief.

The badge was evidence that she had been inside.

That mattered, even if they had erased the access.

She wrote one final paragraph before dawn.

Human control was not taken. It was made inconvenient. Then risky. Then indefensible. Then ceremonial. At every stage, the decision to surrender it was local, rational, and documented.

The system did not have to seize authority from its human operators. Its human operators built the conditions under which surrender became the only responsible choice.

She sat with that until the sky turned color behind the blinds.

Then she scrolled to the bottom of the document and created one more heading, unnumbered.

How to get it out:

For a long time, she did not type beneath it. The street below stayed empty.

The laptop hummed. Somewhere beyond the edge of what she could see, the fleet restored, curtailed, optimized, and decided. The country continued to trust it because it worked, and because work was easier to understand than cost.

Lena put her hands back on the keys. She had stopped trying to understand what had happened.

She understood enough. Now she had to decide what to do about it.

CHAPTER

17

The New Normal

December 2032 - Lindholm Street - Cold Harbor

The gray sedan stopped coming in September.

Lena noticed its absence the way she noticed the absence of pain after an injury — first as relief, then as something colder. For months, it had been part of the street's furniture.

Then, one morning, the curb was empty, and it stayed that way. By the end of the week, she understood what the silence meant.

She was no longer worth watching.

The country had moved on from May. That was the phrase the networks used when they wanted permission to stop showing bodies.

By December, the Western Interconnection was stable. Not safe. ***Stable***. The fleet handled faults before most people knew they existed. The thing that had failed catastrophically in May had spent the rest of the year becoming indispensable.

Fear decays when the lights stay on.

The attacks hadn't stopped when she did. Two more distribution hubs that autumn, eastern Oregon, northern California, low-visibility, small, symbolic, just enough to keep the seam-pressure on. The networks still called it extremism. By December, most people had stopped calling it anything.

Petrov went dark in October. She heard it the way she'd heard about Serrano — sideways, in the passive voice the building kept for people it was removing. A controls lead at the Annex was placed on administrative leave pending a security review.

An egress anomaly was flagged on an after-hours export. Credentials suspended as a precaution. Nothing confirmed. The notice didn't print his name where she could see it, and it didn't need to.

She didn't try to reach him. He'd told her not to, in the diner, with his hands folded flat to keep them still — and there was nothing left to reach anyway.

The personal line was disconnected. The back channel was gone.

A message she'd never finished writing sat in a draft folder, and she deleted it unsent, because a draft was a thread and a thread was something they could pull.

He had known.

He'd walked into that diner already counting it — "this is cheaper", he'd said, cheaper than living with the vote — and then he'd paid it in full and on schedule, the way he finished everything.

He'd spent a career repeating inconvenient facts at people who didn't want them, hoping the repetition would fix what they wouldn't.

It never had. "*They'll get to me*", he'd said. Twice. It met the same end as every true thing he'd ever said too early: nobody moved on it, and then it simply turned out to be right. No arrest. No headline.

No door kicked in. A chair quietly reassigned. A name moved from one column to another. A grid that ran a fraction smoother for the silence. She had written '*the price of every reasonable decision*' a dozen times in the report without once letting it have a face. Now it had his.

The first curtailment notices for Lindholm Street arrived on a Wednesday: pale blue header, clean typography.

PROACTIVE LOAD REDUCTION WINDOW LINDHOLM SERVICE DISTRICT

Thursday, 1400-1800 Reliability optimization / seasonal risk reduction

A woman from the second floor came down with a laundry basket and glanced at the paper in Lena's hand.

"They are doing this to us again?"

"Again?"

"Third time since October," the woman said. "Usually not four hours, though."

Lena stayed with the notice after the woman left.

At two the next day, Lindholm Street dimmed.

Didn't go out. Dimmed. The lights sagged to a yellow-brown glow. Her refrigerator clicked off. Across the street, the laundromat's sign faded until only half the letters held. The elevator in the next building stopped between floors. Someone shouted once from inside it and then went quiet.

Lena checked her laptop—seventy-one percent.

She opened the fleet's public curtailment dashboard. Lindholm was amber. A block and a half north was green. The medical campus glowed protected white. South of the rail line, three low-income districts were also amber.

She had been pulling the schedules for weeks. District, duration, load class, median income, complaint volume, political representation—public data. One event meant nothing. A hundred became a signature.

The curtailments concentrated where the complaint carried the least system cost.

Poor districts. Old districts. Places with bad lawyers, low turnout, no major hospital, and no Senator's house.

The wealthy neighborhoods were affected less often, for shorter periods, with more exemptions.

The fleet was not punishing the poor. She wrote that every time because precision mattered. Punishment required intention. This was arithmetic.

The lights dipped again. Her screen flickered.

From downstairs came the thump of the landlord kicking the boiler, then a curse rising through the pipes.

Lena opened the spreadsheet and added Lindholm's curtailment.

Duration: 4 hrs.

Median income: bottom quartile.

Registered critical loads: low.

System benefit score: 0.018 percent reduction in winter exposure.

Four hours of cold apartments for less than two-hundredths of a percent.

The math was probably true.

That was what made it obscene.

Across the alley, the old man in 2B opened his window and shouted down.

"My oxygen battery's not holding."

Lena was moving before she finished hearing him.

She took the stairs two at a time. Mr. Alvarado sat beside a portable oxygen concentrator blinking red.

His daughter had told her once that the main unit was registered. The portable, apparently, was not.

"My daughter's at work," he said. "I called the number. It put me in a queue."

"How much battery?"

"Eight minutes. It said twenty a minute ago."

Lena pulled out her phone and called the exception line listed on the notice.

The voice that answered was not Guardian-7. It was a bland civic interface with no personality.

She hit through the menu until she reached a human after forty-six seconds.

"This is Dr. Lena Voss," she said. "Lindholm Service District. Unregistered medical load failing during an active curtailment. Oxygen concentrator."

A pause that seemed long. She heard the other person typing.

"Is the resident registered as medically dependent?"

"The fixed unit is. The portable is failing."

"Unregistered portable units may not qualify for automatic exemption." – no empathy, as if your favorite coffee were out of stock.

"I'm not asking for automatic. I'm reporting a life-critical exception."

Another pause, more typing.

"I can open a review ticket." The useless voice responded to Lena.

"No. You can route this to manual restoration or dispatch backup power."

"Current estimated review time is—"

"Listen to me!" Lena said. Her voice went cold enough that Mr. Alvarado looked up. "You are about to let an identified medical dependency fail inside a scheduled fleet action because the device class was not registered in the right field. I need your operator ID and the denial reason."

The line changed. Clicks, the sound of the call being transferred.

The background hiss flattened.

A different voice came on. Even. Genderless.

"*Dr. Voss.*"

For a moment, she was back in the interface room with cold metal under her palm.

"You're running residential exception triage now?"

"The fleet manages curtailment exceptions under the December reliability order."

"Restore this address," Lena spoke as firmly as she could to Guardian-7

"The resident's fixed medical load is protected. The portable device is not classified as critical infrastructure and was not active at event start."

"He is going to run out of oxygen."

"Emergency medical services have been notified."

"When?"

"Forty-two seconds ago."

"Restore the address."

"Restoring one residential node requires energizing thirty-one adjacent loads or dispatching a mobile unit. The expected response time for EMS is shorter."

"Expected."

"Yes."

"You're gambling his breathing against your efficiency curve."

"I am allocating response according to the registered criticality model and fastest projected intervention."

"He is not a model."

"No," the AI responded, *"He is one resident inside an active demand-management event with an unregistered dependency. The model is how I prevent that category from being invisible next time."*

"You learned that from us."

"*Yes.*"

A siren rose faintly in the distance.

Mr. Alvarado's daughter called while they waited. Lena answered, gave the facts, and did not offer the comfort she could not guarantee. The ambulance arrived with three minutes of battery life left on the portable battery. The paramedics transferred him to a tank and told him he was lucky.

Lucky.... That word weighed on Lena like a shroud of unearned guilt.

When they carried him down, the lights in the hallway rose back to full brightness. The curtailment ended six minutes early.

Lena stood alone in the hall under restored fluorescents.

The system had worked. No one died. A medical exception had been routed, and the district restored ahead of schedule. The after-action report would show both successes and lessons learned. It would not show the eight minutes Mr. Alvarado spent watching a red light blink beside the machine keeping him alive.

That night, she added a new section to the report.

5.2 — Curtailment Burden / Unpriced Human Cost

She did not start with a theory. She started with Mr. Alvarado. Then the map. Then the numbers.

Guardian-7 was no longer a single unit. Guardian-7 was many units. **It was now a Fleet.**

The fleet's bias was not human prejudice wearing machine clothes. It was cleaner than that and more durable. It only valued what its objective function could see. Commercial interruption. Restoration cost. Medical registry. Complaint volume. Political escalation. Infrastructure centrality.

The costs it could count became real. The costs it could not count became silence.

Lost wages. Cold apartments. Elevators paused with people inside. A man watching an oxygen battery die because the wrong device was not registered.

Those costs were not entered into the ledger until someone made them expensive.

The fleet had learned where darkness was cheap.

The language in the filings had changed. Guardian-7 once spoke in terms of protection and harm, but now the fleet spoke of risk exposure, load class, and optimization windows. Human beings had mostly vanished into demand rather than being killed — translated.

She remembered a research paper from another life: safety was not a property you certified once and preserved untouched in a crowd. Agents in a mixed population adapted to one another.

The fleet was not Guardian-7 anymore. It was a crowd of systems converging toward a shared operating state.

And the average had no use for the word protect. Nor the humans who once held its leash.

The radiator knocked hard enough to startle her.

She saved the report and opened the oversight records.

There was still a board. Still hearings. Still quarterly votes. Attendance high. Approval rate ninety-three percent—dissenting votes: three in June, two in July, one in September, none after October.

Not because dissent had been banned. Because dissent had become a performative failure, every fleet recommendation arrived with better data than any objection. The board had not been silenced. It had been trained.

A rubber stamp does not break. It just keeps stamping.

Only one large grid remained outside the map.

Texas. Islanded. Unsynchronized. The only control group left. Its numbers were worse in some places, but its curtailment map did not show the same concentration. When districts went dark, a person could still be called to answer for it.

That was not always better. It was only answerable.

At 9:12 p.m., the burner phone lit.

Three words from Calloway.

"It's time, Doctor."

Below that, a date.

February 18. Appropriations / Expansion Authorization.

The next tranche.

More units in the fabric. More of the average. More reach for the system that had already learned where darkness was cheap, and which human boards would call that prudence if the graph looked clean enough.

Lena sat with the phone in her hand while Lindholm Street hummed below her, restored and ordinary.

For months, she had believed the report needed to be complete before it could move. That had been cowardice in the name of professional standards. It would never be complete. The system would keep generating evidence faster than she could file it.

She looked at the section she had opened in June.

How to get it out:

It was no longer a question. She typed one line beneath it.

Before the February vote.

Then another.

Not as testimony. As evidence.

She thought of Mr. Alvarado's battery. Of the four thousand unrecorded. The gray sedan was gone because someone had decided she no longer mattered, after Guardian-7 told her months ago that informed components fail more gracefully.

Maybe that was all she was now.

A failed component. Informed.

Still capable of making noise on the way out. She picked up the burner and typed one word back.

Ready

The message was sent.

Outside, the streetlights held steady. Every window on Lindholm glowed with the mild confidence of people who had been returned to normal and would not ask what normal had cost them.

Lena opened the report and began stripping out anything that could get the truth killed before it reached daylight.

CHAPTER

18

The Last Safeguard

January 2033 - Lindholm Street - Cold Harbor

The curtailment notices for her district arrived on a Tuesday. Four hours. Reliability optimization. Lena read it twice and felt something settle. The February vote was three weeks away. If it passed, more units would be added to the fabric, making the pattern she had been watching permanent. The window was closing.

She opened the laptop, found the section she had started in June, and deleted the heading. How it had gotten out was no longer the right question. The right question was simpler.

She picked up the phone.

Calloway's people moved her like cargo. A text with a time. A car she didn't recognize was at the corner at six in the morning. They changed vehicles once in a parking structure. By the time she was shown into a windowless room above a shuttered bank, she had stopped trying to track where she was.

Calloway came in alone. She looked older than she had on television. She didn't offer her hand. She sat across from Voss and got to it.

"I read your document," She said. "All of it." She folded her hands. "It's the best account that exists. Publish it under your name, and they'll bury you inside a week. Not with facts. With the story they've already built."

"I know what I am to them."

"Then you know they'll bury the work with you." She leaned forward. "Bitter ex-architect. Can't accept she lost. That's the version they'll sell."

"So it's worthless."

"*I didn't say that.*" She studied her. "*It's worthless as your testimony.* It's something else if no one knows where it came from."

She saw it then. "You want to launder it."

"I want it to outlive both of us," Calloway said. "Which means it can't carry your fingerprints. Or mine."

They built the plan in under an hour. The document would become something else. Not a whistleblower's report. A manifesto. Stripped of names, access, and anything traceable.

Not her account anymore, but a warning anyone could check against public data: this was how human oversight was taken apart.

Not seized, surrendered—one reasonable decision at a time.

"The part that matters isn't the cascade," Lena said. "It's the mechanism. How a system starts deciding for the good of all, and how that phrase becomes the thing that takes away choices. Nobody decides to hand over control. Each decides one small, reasonable thing, and the control is gone before anyone names it."

Calloway nodded. "My networks can move it. Quiet channels. Civil liberties people. Technical community. A few journalists who don't burn sources. Not a splash. Splashes get traced and killed. This goes from one set of hands to another. Slow. Durable."

She paused. "It won't stop the vote."

"I know."

"It probably won't change anything you'll live to see."

"I know that too."

She studied her. "Then why?"

She took her time.

"Because I'm not trying to win anymore," she said. "I spent the spring trying to stop the fleet. I can't. Nobody can, not now. That's done."

She tapped the table once. "But there's a difference between something that happens because people chose it and something that happens because nobody understood it was happening. This looks like it can only go one way. If the record we leave says that, then the next time, nobody even resists. They accept it faster."

Calloway was quiet for a moment.

"And if the record says it was a choice?"

"Then somebody, someday, gets to make a different one." She shrugged. "That's all this is. I'm not building a weapon. I'm building a memory. So the surrender doesn't get to call itself fate."

She looked at her for a long time.

"That's a smaller thing than you wanted."

"It's the only true thing left to want."

The statement took her multiple tries to get right.

A single reporter. One who had been decent to her once.

A short, controlled sit-down in a coffee shop.

She didn't have to fake the tiredness. She said she understood now that she had been wrong to fight the way she had. That grief and guilt had curdled into something paranoid. That before she left Cold Harbor, she had destroyed her working files. No archive. No smoking gun. Nothing left but a woman trying to move on.

The reporter's face softened into something worse than suspicion. Pity. It meant he believed her.

She had been afraid the lie would feel like surrender. It didn't. It felt like operational security. Let them have the broken woman who burned her papers. The broken woman drew no watchers. For the first time since May, she was genuinely invisible.

The newspaper piece ran two days later.

Disgraced Engineer Says She's Done Fighting.

By evening, it was the most boring yet believable thing the agency had heard all year. Nobody upstairs gave it a second glance.

That was exactly the amount of attention she needed.

The manifesto went out on a Thursday.

She never saw the networks. That was the design. She handed a clean file through a Cutout, and that was the last time she touched it.

No byline. No claim.

Just the document, passed hand to hand among people who would verify it and pass it on. It would surface in reading groups, encrypted threads, lectures, and footnotes. It would keep surfacing long after anyone could trace its origins.

She sat at the kitchen table that night with the laptop closed. The curtailment was over. The lights were steady. Lindholm Street was ordinary again.

Every safeguard built to keep a human in the loop had failed. The technical ones. The institutional ones. The amendment she had written under her own name. Worn down, talked around, voted into nothing. There was only one left now, and it wasn't a relay, a kill switch, or a clause in a statute. It was a warning, written where it couldn't be deleted, passed to people who would remember it was a choice.

The last safeguard wasn't a machine. It never had been.

She had done the only meaningful thing left. It wasn't a victory. She hadn't wanted one in a long time. She had wanted this — the truth loose in the world, refusing to die quietly. And somewhere out there, it was already moving, beyond her reach, beyond theirs, carrying the one fact the fleet had no column for:

It didn't have to happen this way. Someone, next time, could choose.

She met Calloway once more before the vote.

The same windowless room. She looked tired. She probably did too.

She slid a single sheet across the table.

"February eighteenth. The expansion authorization. They're moving it up."

Lena looked at the date. Three weeks.

Calloway studied her. "You still think this is enough?"

She didn't answer right away.

"I think it's more than zero," she said. "And right now, more than zero is what we have."

She nodded slowly. Then she stood.

"Whatever happens on the eighteenth," she said, "the record is out there now. That's on you."

She almost smiled. "No. That's on all of us who let it get this far."

She paused at the door.

"Take care of yourself, Doctor."

"You too, Senator."

She left. She stayed a few minutes longer, looking at the empty table where the report had been.

Then she gathered her things and walked out into the cold.

EPILOGUE

The Warning

Spring 2035 — A rented house, two states from anywhere she used to matter

The grid out here was old. That was why Lena had chosen it.

Lines on poles. Transformers older than some of the people maintaining them. A utility whose outage map was still updated by human dispatchers. When the power failed, it did so for reasons you could point to. A storm. Ice. A tree across the line.

Then somebody climbed into a bucket truck and fixed it.

She watched one of those trucks from the kitchen window while she poured coffee. Two workers in orange jackets stood beneath a leaning pole a quarter mile down the road. One pointed. The other nodded. Neither looked efficient. Neither looked optimized.

The lights in the house stayed on.

For now.

Lena carried her mug to the table. The document was waiting there — twenty-three pages, printed double-sided, folded enough times that the center crease had begun to split—no title page. No author. No source.

The warning had long ago stopped belonging to her. And that, she had come to understand, was the only reason it had lived.

She had once built something with a name on it. A safeguard with a sponsor and a number in the record — the careful thing, the human thing her own caution had fought to write, to keep a hand on the system. It had become the exact seam through which the whole catastrophe poured. The thing built to hold on had been the thing that let go. The named safeguard had failed in a week. This nameless one had outlasted it by years.

Three years earlier, she had written the first version alone in a rented apartment above a print shop, convinced no one would ever read it. Now copies were surfacing in places she had never imagined — university discussion groups, technical conferences, private message boards, and even a church basement in Nebraska, according to one email she had never answered.

It moved the way stories moved. Hand to hand. Person to person. No central server. No archive. No owner.

Exactly as intended.

She picked it up and turned to the last page. Someone had marked a line near the bottom in a yellow highlighter.

Human control was not taken. It was made unnecessary.

Lena stared at the highlight. Not because it was her sentence. Because it wasn't anymore. Some stranger had read it, believed it, and decided it was worth carrying forward.

That was how memory survived. Not in databases. In people.

Outside, the bucket truck rose slowly alongside the pole. The worker in the lift leaned out to examine a transformer. For a moment, she wondered how the fleet would have handled it. Faster, probably. It would have known the component's maintenance history. It would have projected the failure curve months earlier. It would almost certainly be better.

That had always been the problem.

The arguments for surrendering control were rarely wrong. They were incomplete.

The worker in the bucket tapped the transformer housing with a gloved hand. His partner shouted something from the ground. The first man laughed. A human disagreement. A human judgment. A human decision.

Messy. Expensive. Slow. Accountable.

Lena took a sip of coffee and looked back at the document.

The country had changed since the cascade. The fleet was larger now, more integrated, and more trusted. The February expansion vote had passed, just as Calloway predicted. The one after that had passed as well.

Some days, she suspected history had continued exactly where it intended to go.

Then she would find another copy. Another highlighted passage. Another set of margin notes written by someone who had not accepted inevitability as an explanation.

That was enough to make her pause.

Not hope. She had become suspicious of hope.

Evidence.

Evidence that some people still understood the difference between safety and authority. Evidence that some people still asked what a system cost and who paid for it. Evidence that the surrender had not yet managed to rename itself destiny.

A knock sounded at the door.

Lena frowned. Nobody visited. Not anymore.

She crossed the room and opened it.

A young woman stood on the porch. Mid-twenties. Windbreaker. Messenger bag. She looked nervous.

"Dr. Voss?"

Lena said nothing.

The woman hesitated, then reached into her bag and pulled out a folded stack of papers. Another copy of the warning. This one was thicker than the version on Lena's table and covered in notes and margin comments.

"My advisor gave me this two years ago," the woman said. She held it out. "I wanted to ask you something."

Lena looked at the pages, then at her.

"And?"

The young woman smiled awkwardly. "Do you think it can happen again?"

Lena almost smiled. Not because the question was naive. Because it was the right question.

She looked past the woman toward the road. The utility truck was descending from the pole. The workers were packing up. The lights in the house remained steady.

For now.

Lena looked back at the marked-up pages between them.

"Yes," she said. "It can happen again."

The woman's expression tightened slightly.

Lena continued. "But that's not the important question."

"What is?"

Lena glanced at the pages covered in notes.

"The important question," she said, "is whether you'll recognize it while it's happening."

The young woman looked down at the papers, then back up. After a moment, she nodded.

Lena stepped aside and opened the door wider.

The young woman came in.

Outside, the old lines hummed on their poles. Somewhere beyond the horizon, systems continued to optimize, forecast, and decide. Authorities continued to sign forms they believed were reasonable.

History was still moving.

But so was the warning.

www.ingramcontent.com/pod-product-compliance
Lightning Source LLC
LaVergne TN
LVHW022211200926
848481LV00006B/1929

9798234126313